MW01138054

the secret life of *it girls*

dakota lane

ginee seo books > atheneum books for young readers > new york london toronto sydney

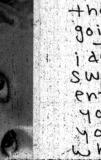

it pop, so no m
know u got 2 min

in yall sum love

i am the girl who y
learned not to sho

am the girl who y
athetic, scary, reta

am the girl who s
your chatter break

PROFILE
BLOG
PICS / VIDS
FRIENDS
ENEMIES
MESSAGE

"somewhere over th

[more photos]

sweet sixteen

*the romance
of tristan and chloe*

how to survive a solo weekend

baby it girl

10   11   12   13

How an It Girl Became an Out Girl

LINDSIE:
Obviously they wouldn't be treating us like this if Jaz hadn't posted the pictures of Kristyn and Tyler.
But none of it was Jaz's fault. Jaz was the one who got most hurt.

If you were a normal person and you went on mydamnspace and happened to see the pictures,
you'd be like: gross, thank you so much for sharing this random porn moment.
But you wouldn't dwell on it.
You'd click onto the next thing and just keep going.
You would not be overly shocked.

SHEA:
Hello, if Jaz knew that parents would stalk us online and see the pictures, she wouldn't have posted
the pictures. This kind of thing happens all the time, but we didn't know it would happen to us.

Basically, the parents are still freaked and they're trying to blame this entire crisis on someone,
just because they don't want to know what their perfect children are really up to.
And guess whose clique is said to be the cause of the scandal?

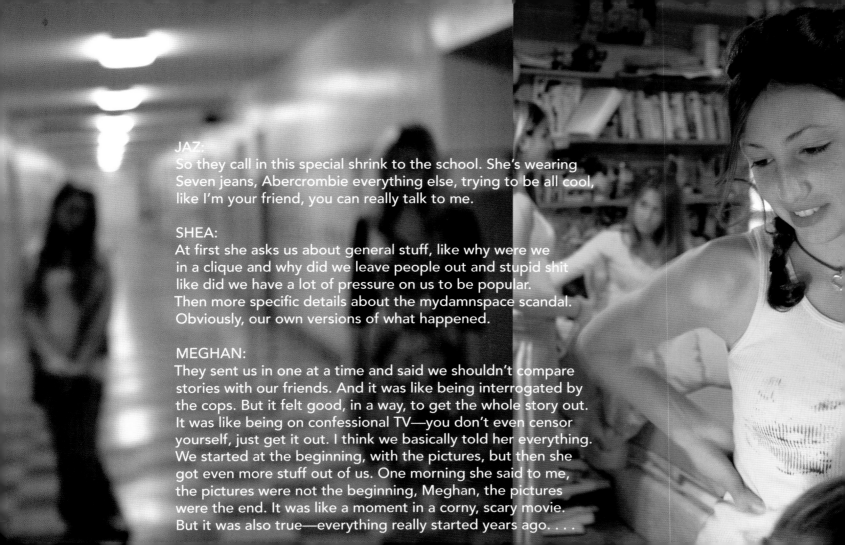

JAZ:
So they call in this special shrink to the school. She's wearing
Seven jeans, Abercrombie everything else, trying to be all cool,
like I'm your friend, you can really talk to me.

SHEA:
At first she asks us about general stuff, like why were we
in a clique and why did we leave people out and stupid shit
like did we have a lot of pressure on us to be popular.
Then more specific details about the mydamnspace scandal.
Obviously, our own versions of what happened.

MEGHAN:
They sent us in one at a time and said we shouldn't compare
stories with our friends. And it was like being interrogated by
the cops. But it felt good, in a way, to get the whole story out.
It was like being on confessional TV—you don't even censor
yourself, just get it out. I think we basically told her everything.
We started at the beginning, with the pictures, but then she
got even more stuff out of us. One morning she said to me,
the pictures were not the beginning, Meghan, the pictures
were the end. It was like a moment in a corny, scary movie.
But it was also true—everything really started years ago. . . .

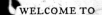

WELCOME TO

chez chez

THESE ARE MY:

- PROFILE
- BLOG
- PICS / VIDS
- FRIENDS
- ENEMIES
- MESSAGES

"no regrets"

[more photos]

female, 15 years
we do it better in,
anytown, USA

last online: today

POST 1-63 OF 63

:LINDSIE

WHO WE ARE.

Basically, Shea and I were best friends since preschool, got our belly buttons pierced for our twelfth birthdays, survived good times and bad. We hooked up with Jaz, Meghan, Kristyn, who had a clique since junior high. Kristyn split off and Meghan's the only one still talking to the biatch. We are THE POSSE.

(Kristyn)

(Meghan, Lindsie, Jaz, Shea)

THE STORY OF THE TRASHED (AND TRASHY) SENIOR AND HOW SHE GAVE US OUR NAME.

 :LINDSIE

We always find shit that makes us laugh, even in the most pathetic circumstances. Like this party we went to last summer out in West Tilton. We get there and pretty much within seconds, some senior girl's boyfriend is totally hitting on Shea. And he didn't know Shea was like fourteen. The guys always go for Shea first — she's lil and cute and has big boobs — or Jaz, she has the whole deluxe bitch package — long hair, knows how to dress, etc. Sadly, I am the one they talk to for an hour first. And Meghan — she's beautiful but guys always think she's too serious to have fun with.

Anyway, the girl whose boyfriend it was—she was so messed up. It was this huge keg party and the place was trashed and it was so smoky you just had to breathe to get high. The girl was so trashed she had actually taken off her shirt and was dancing in her freakin' bra — and not even a cute bra, this big shiny ho bra, it was dark in there and her bra was totally glowing. Anyway, she saw her boy hookin' up with Shea and she was buggin'. She basically grabs Shea by the hair and tells her to get the hell out and to take her whole pussy Posse with her.

Of course I missed a lot of this because the beer was gone and I was drinking this sweet red liquor and I was in the bathroom trying not to be sick. Shea helped me out, as usual.

(Lindsie (sick) and Shea)

The next day when we were trying to get to the mall or whatever, trying to figure out rides, I'm on the phone with Jaz and she's like what's the Posse doing today? She said it all sarcastic, but it stuck.
For months now we're like what's the Posse doing.
So that's how the clique got its name. Everyone knew about the Posse, we were all over mydamnspace. We were notorious — in a good way. And then — fast forward to the winter dance.

HOW THINGS SUDDENLY GOT OUT OF CONTROL THE FATEFUL NIGHT OF THE WINTER DANCE.

:SHEA

So Jaz and Tyler have a big fight that afternoon and break up for like the fiftieth time. She's a mess so I stay home with her.
Lindsie's in bed with the flu.
That leaves Meghan. Who goes to the dance. Who apparently partied with Kristyn afterwards. Meghan says she didn't know what Kristyn was up to with Tyler, but we do not believe her.
So right after the dance everything becomes raw chaos.
Kristyn posts her little fake pictures of her and Tyler dancing. (At the dance, before they went into his car.)
Tyler and Kristyn hook up all weekend at her dad's.

Jaz finds out and I don't know why, takes Tyler back.
Then Jaz posts the disgusting pictures of Kristyn and Tyler that she got off Tyler's cell.
Then Chloe Rybecki's brat sister sees them and next thing all the parents are spazzing out about everyone's mydamnspace pages.
There's off-the-chain psychodrama still going on and THE POSSE is still notorious, all over mydamnspace. This morning someone posted a whole page saying: **the posse = rancid offspring-eating bitches.**
I mean, wtf?
Whoever said it, they're probably worse than us.
Everyone's a hypocrite.
If you check out what everyone else is up to, it's obvious we're not that bad.
No one is innocent.

HAIR, HOBAGS, AND THE PERKS OF BEING IN A CLIQUE.

:SHEA

You get up in the morning and you're pumped—it's almost like being a star — you care about how you look because you know people are looking at you.

But no one's going around saying wow, I'm in a group, I'm officially cool, I am soooo popular.
We don't leave kids out, or not talk to them because they're not cool enough. We talk to whoever talks to us. What's annoying are these pathetic losers who are always like, oooh, where did you get those cool clothes. And I'm always like, hey, I shop at the same stores you do, just get a style. Jaz is worse, She's like, it's couture — look for it on the sale rack at Marshall's, good luck.

:LINDSIE

     People are jealous, obviously. Even the teachers pamper us — this one science teacher basically showed us this empty room where we go to hang out between classes, change our clothes, etc. Like we are stars. People are always like how are you the way you are?

:SHEA

     Or they want to know about your hair. I'm sorry, but I spend two hundred dollars a month to make it look like this, because money is always a factor — but hello, anyone can afford a straightening iron and product, so there's no excuse.

HOW WE DEAL WITH PATHETIC LOSERS.

:JAZ

The worst are the pathetic stalker groupies; they stare at you longingly, like oh please pay attention to me — but we don't say anything rude to them.

They always sit near us for some reason and we say things to them, we're not stuck up. And they actually aren't that nice to us, either. They aren't that lively. Actually, the worst are the people who don't hang out with anyone and don't say anything at all. They scare me.

(Kristyn and her weird gang)

 :LINDSIE

Maybe we don't try to hang out with random people or make them part of THE POSSE, but A) we're not trying to be like Mother Teresa or someone and B) that would be so fake, trying to hang out all the time with someone you have nothing in common with.

:JAZ

I hate fake people more than anything. No wait, I hate hobags and dykey losers and THEN fake people, in that order.

Just kidding! I would never be that harsh.

:MEGHAN

A BIATCH — IN A GOOD WAY.

Yes, Jaz is that harsh, that's what I've been realizing.
She's not a nice person. It's so typical that she would create all this drama and then stand back with a little smile and be like, What? Who, me?

:SHEA

Jaz is just naturally bossy, and a bitch, in a good way — and she knows it. And she is freakin hilarious. You're like home alone avoiding your homework and then you go on mydamnspace and Jaz sends you a message like: Quit pouting, you big emo dyke, you're making my hard-on wilt.

:LINDSIE

I don't know if Jaz was over-the-top with what she did. It's all perspective, it's all who you're listening to. And I'm not listening to what people are saying because Jaz is my friend and if you listen to what everyone's saying you're basically a sheep.

:MEGHAN

WHO YOU CALLING A DRAMA WHORE?

Lindsie is in denial. Jaz devastated and humiliated Kristyn with those pictures. And Tyler is an idiot. And he's like — I was freakin' high, don't blame me. Like he was forced to do it, like Kristyn gave him date rape drugs and then made him use his cell cam at gunpoint. And if Kristyn was so horrible, then why did Tyler spend the whole weekend basically acting like he was into her? He did not deserve one hour or one second with her. He's perfect for Jaz, they're like the couple from hell. They're like drama vampires.

(Jaz and Tyler (on)

(off)

(maybe?))

:LINDSIE

Everyone's a drama whore, even though the first thing people say in their profiles is I hate drama. Like, just admit you love it. Even those series books, even the reality shows, how boring would they be without gossip, backstabbing, etc.

:SHEA

I get this feeling that Meghan is a fake. She's the kinda girl who parties but she never loses that uptight look. And wtf is up with her and Kristyn? You can't exactly have a friend who tells you that she's not into drama and doesn't want to get involved. And then she's secretly hanging out with your enemy, I mean, wtf is up with that?

KRISTYN'S DEAL.

:LINDSIE

It's so weird if you look at how we were doing everything with Kristyn like one year ago and suddenly she's this person who hates us and she has all these people involved who don't even know us and they hate us too. I couldn't trust her after she left, because she knew all our secrets. I don't get why Meghan still likes her.

:SHEA

You pretty much need a chart to figure out who was friends with who and who hooked up with who and how it keeps changing. Someone's always leaving, like Kristyn — she and Jaz had this little rift so she basically started hanging out with these indie freaks she used to know.

:JAZ

We were soooooo close when we were little but I can't even remember why. Prolly because of our mothers being friends. Just because you bond over ice cream sundaes, SpongeBob, afternoons in the video arcade, I mean why would we still be together?

 :MEGHAN

It is such bs when people say that Kristyn drifted off and went back to her old friends. She was too close to Jaz, that's what happened. Jaz makes you get close to her. She's very seductive, She's got this energy that pulls you right in. She flirts with everyone, even girls. Some people are always hugging you, kissing on the mouth, touching you while they talk. She's like that. If you really want to know the dirt, all the dirt, Kristyn didn't just get bored with us and start hanging out with those random people. I know exactly the night, a year ago, when she and Jaz basically broke up.

PLOT THICKENS AT THE COED SLEEPOVER.

:LINDSIE

We were at Brandon's house having a coed sleepover. It was this bizarro time over winter break when we somehow had our parents convinced that we were all innocent, that we were all just friends and that it would be like gross or something if we were to like hook up with our friends, who just happened to be boys. We were like, don't you trust us? You raised us, now you should just trust us. I mean Shea's and Jaz's moms are cool and they let them have boys over but my mom is more strict and Meghan's is the worst. But this night we convinced all of them to let us do this.

:SHEA

So Brandon has this attic and his mother was all cute, making us brownies, checking on us, telling us to leave the door open. But eventually she fell asleep. So we had this freak party, it was wack because it was silent, I mean completely silent, we were even laughing without making noise, it was like we were on drugs. Well we were smoking — we leaned so far out the window so the smell wouldn't come in the house — and it was ironic, because Brandon actually got the pot from his mother, and we were hiding it from her. Some of the kids were saying just blow the smoke under your mom's door and she'll be so out of it she won't care.

 :JAZ

    All I really remember about that night is the way everyone was hanging out the window — like Steff Borsellino almost literally fell out the window, but that's another story. It was such a fun night, and we were drinking but it was like we were seriously tripping because there was no music, etc., and some people were seriously hooking up. The only light was coming from the moon. You could see plenty, though.

(Lindsie (tripping)   and wtf??)

 :LINDSIE

    At one point some of the girls were hooking up with girls, nothing serious, it's not like it's planned, it's just hott. For like two seconds or whatever, guys like it. It's lame, I know, but when you get drunk you do shit like that. It's a joke.

So something happened with Jaz and Kristyn. The usual stuff, but in the morning Brandon was trying to get into Jaz's pants. He crawled into her bed but she just wanted to sleep, too much partying. So he started as a joke to say all this shit about maybe she was a lesbo, maybe she'd rather be with Kristyn. So Jaz was laughing but not Kristyn. Instead of laughing it off, which she should have, Kristyn got into all this stuff about homophobia.

:JAZ

For some reason Kristyn went bipolar that morning, I could never really figure out why. Maybe she needs medication.

:SHEA

PEER PRESSURE, WOOT-WOOT.

The problem with Kristyn is she gets too serious, she goes like psychotic. So what could Jaz do, confess her deep love for Kristyn and ask all of us to their gay wedding? So Jaz was like eww, you practically raped me last night, you big dyke. So Kristyn had this big sulk fit and got her father to pick her up early and after that we were completely not allowed coed sleepovers. All Kristyn's fault, obviously. So she just stopped hanging out with us. And she was suddenly with this other group.

:LINDSIE

They weren't goth, they weren't punk, they were attention whores: they did a protest march in the halls and got suspended for smoking in the bathroom. They made a big deal about making a movie; they did it all of last semester and it was really annoying. They thought they were so off-the-chain amazing.

:JAZ

Sometimes people change so much that you almost want to be like, excuse me, are you Kristyn or is that someone borrowing your body? So if you keep asking me if I miss Kristyn, I'd have to say — which Kristyn? Because the one she is now is not someone you would miss, unless you're into freak shows.

:SHEA

I think she was really badly influenced by those people. Like peer pressure, woot-woot, but there really is peer pressure. Our friend Ben who used to hang out with us all the time started hanging out with Kristyn's group and seriously, in just one day he was wearing eyeliner and black nail polish. It's like they infected him.

We didn't even care what Kristyn was doing with these people. It was boring. They were lame. We would prolly have started to ignore her but then one night we see her at this party and she's got a different personality.

:JAZ

HOW EXACTLY DOES KRISTYN WORK IT?

Just when we got used to Kristyn wearing all those ill-concept, raggy outfits — she shows up in extreme slut wear. Everyone was crowding around her like she had accomplished something major. After that she tried to work it, at every party, it was like she woke up one morning and said hey, I just realized I'm a slut, and I'm going for the gusto!

:LINDSIE

　　We all got in the habit of being obsessed about it — like what is that bitch wearing today? I guess we followed Jaz's attitude about Kristyn, but it's not like we don't have our own eyes and our own mind.

:SHEA

　　Everyone always waits to see what kind of sick thing she's going to do next. Slutty girls are entertaining to watch.

:LINDSIE

　　It's pretty obvious what Kristyn does when you're at a party or

whatever. First she gets really drunk, I mean she's walking but her eyes are freakin' out of it. She might be the type exaggerating how high she is just so she can hit on anyone she wants. And then she gets hyper focused on some guy. and even if he is seriously not interested she will not stop until he's hooking up with her, even if she has to literally pull him off somewhere.
When she dances it's different from everyone else, I can't explain it, it's like she gets all intense and like she's putting on a show. She does not get at all how she looks when she does that, or she wouldn't have put those pics of her and Tyler from that night on her mydamnspace.
She must have thought it was so romantic or something instead of the spectacle that it was.

But Meghan stayed friends with her, I don't even know why.

(Kristyn and Tyler)

:MEGHAN

LOSER, SLUT, OR LUCKY GENETICS?

She's interesting, she's not typical. I'd been friends with her since we were little and suddenly everyone in the group was trashing her. It wasn't right. She added me to her space, so we talked online. Not a big deal.

:JAZ

Meghan is sucked in by Kristyn because Kristyn is needy. Meghan doesn't get that the needier you are the more of a loser you are. You don't walk into a room and look around to see who's noticing you. That's what Kristyn does.

People are really, really drawn to me. Sorry if it sounds conceited, but it's all about attitude. It's not the clothes or how good your tan is. If you feel like a star, people treat you like a star.

:SHEA

It's not exactly a bitch attitude, it's more like life is fun and I own it. What's wrong with that? I wore flip-flops all winter because I wanted to, because it felt hott, but someone else could do it and their feet could look all blue and pasty, yuck. If you have confidence, you can suck your thumb in class, if you want. That could be hott. Everyone wants you to be all emo and lame just because they are.

Jaz has an edge, but that's her trademark.

:MEGHAN

Jaz and Shea definitely have intense attitude, but, if anything, Kristyn is actually the one who naturally attracts guys. She has this softness that Jaz doesn't have. They say her clothes are slutty but that's an exaggeration. I think their obsession with Kristyn comes from jealousy.

:JAZ

Kristyn's whole situation is actually sad. I would feel sorry for her, but the girl stabbed me in the back. She hooked up with Tyler the same weekend we broke up, come on. She knew we were gonna get back together, we always fight and get back together. And then she acts like she's a victim, like she's so perfect and always being hurt by us. Everything we did was REALITY — and she deserved to be exposed.

:LINDSIE

And too bad Meghan was trying to cover up for Kristyn or she could have helped us.

:SHEA

IS MEGHAN A BACKSTABBER OR A DANCE ADDICT?

I first started thinking Meghan was a fake when I found out she was at that dance and she didn't even tell us she saw Tyler dancing with Kristyn.

:MEGHAN

Sorry if I was actually dancing at the dance and not doing my full-time job as spy for Jaz! I did see Tyler hanging out with Kristyn but I didn't see them go out to his car or anything. I didn't even know she was into him, except when I saw her dancing with him. She was buzzed and her friend was taking pictures of them dancing, but it didn't seem like anything that serious.

:LINDSIE

Meghan is actually worse than people think she is. Yeah she saw Kristyn dancing with Tyler — but she also knew that Kristyn was hooking up with Tyler that weekend. This is how I know: the morning after the dance, I called Meghan's house and her mom said — Meghan's still sleeping she got home really late last night. And I didn't say oh I thought the dance was over at midnight because I didn't want to get Meghan in trouble in case she was out partying, but then her mom goes: yeah, Meghan was hanging out with Kristyn after the dance.

:MEGHAN

Shea and Jaz don't even know that after the dance, I got a ride home with someone's sister and Kristyn was in the back of the car.

At first it was awkward but she had some smoke and she was like let's go to the beach. She was in a good mood, she'd just hooked up with Tyler, in his car! Which kind of makes me sick now, but I didn't know that then.

I actually called my mom and said look I'm going to the beach with Kristyn and she was cool with it because she still likes Kristyn, they were really close when we were all hanging out back in the day. My mom was actually thrilled I called even though it was late. She's always saying I should just tell her exactly what I'm doing and confide in her and trust her if I want her to trust me, blah, blah.

 :LINDSIE

When I found out that Meghan was stabbing Jaz in the back — by hanging out with Kristyn at the dance — I probably should have told somebody. But Jaz was already a mess and I just didn't say anything and then it got too late. It would have been awkward.

:MEGHAN   **MEGHAN AND KRISTYN DO SOME BONDING.**

So Kristyn and me were on the beach, for like five seconds. It was a freezing, windy night. So we walked to this all-night place. We had a great time, I didn't expect that. It had been so long since I had an actual conversation about real things — with Lindsie, almost, but not really. We were fooling around a lot and there were weird people out at that time of night, staring, so we left before they threw us out. We live in the same neighborhood so we walked about twenty blocks to our houses.

That's when she told me that she thought she had this kind of deep connection with Tyler, her exact words. I don't even know how she could think that, there is nothing deep about that boy. She told me they were going to hang out at her dad's house the next day, that her dad was going to be gone all weekend. I was kind of shocked. I knew I should tell someone. But I'd just spent all night talking to her. So I did nothing.

:SHEA

When you look back at that weekend, it's obvious Kristyn was plotting to get Tyler. And of course he fell for it, he's a guy, what guy can turn down a ho? It just shows you how low she is — you just don't seduce someone's boyfriend.

:JAZ

Here's the deal even though it's obvious: she wasn't just screwing him, she was screwing me. She wants to be me so bad she'd settle for my leftovers.

:MEGHAN

Kristyn is insecure and sensitive — not an aggressive bitch like everyone's saying. She really thought something was going to happen with her and Tyler, and it's not like he was married to Jaz, they were always breaking up, Jaz doesn't own him. In a way, I get her more than anyone in our group but it's not like I'm going to leave the group to hang out with her.

MEGHAN HAS ISSUES.

:SHEA

What I don't get is why Meghan keeps hanging around with us. It just shows you how Jaz is such a basically good person that she even freakin' puts up with Meghan.

:MEGHAN

It's hard to stop hanging out with a clique. For one thing you automatically know what you are going to do every day. You know who you're going to sit with at lunch, you know who you're going to bitch to when you're bored after school and hanging on mydamnspace avoiding homework. On the weekends, etc., you get the picture. It sounds shallow but it's somehow not. It's like they are more than your friends. It sometimes almost doesn't matter if you hate them, they're like your family.

(THE POSSE, before the drama)

But even if I decided to break out — look what happened with Kristyn. If you leave a clique, the old clique basically rips you apart for the rest of your life. Jaz, Shea and even Lindsie are so freakin' obsessed with Kristyn, they are constantly analyzing what she is wearing, how she is acting. It's like they're trying to prove something hateful about her.

:SHEA

PUBLIC HUMILIATION, ON A SCALE OF ONE TO TEN.

We haven't told one lie about Kristyn. Jaz went for mass destruction, but anyone would have been freakin' pissed. I mean this is your boyfriend and here is this ho saying I heart Tyler and putting those pics up. She made them all arty like they were scenes from a movie. Gabe or someone was taking them. Kristyn didn't know about the other pics, the ones Tyler took when they hooked up in his car after the party. Or maybe she did know.

:MEGHAN

Kristyn was seriously seriously hurt by Tyler. Her father was gone that weekend and Tyler was over at her house the whole time. She had never even had a real boyfriend before, just guys she hooked up with, and he was supposedly so sweet to her. They were like cooking for each other.

They rented Molly Ringwald movies, come on, that is so not what you do with someone you don't like. Unless he was trying to make Jaz jealous, that's what Jaz thinks, but like I said, Tyler isn't that deep, he wouldn't spend all that time with someone and freakin' cook freakin' vegetarian lasagne and sleep in their bed and they even took a bubble bath, how cute is that? But seriously not cute when you think of how it ended up.

Those pictures were pretty graphic, it was pretty gross. No one really knows if he actually showed them to Jaz when they got back together or if she just was looking at his cell but he should have erased them.

:LINDSIE

Meghan is always talking about Kristyn's feelings. But can you imagine how Jaz felt when she first saw the pics that Kristyn put on mydamnspace?

We were over at Shea's house the day we saw them. I was lying on the bed with Meghan. At first we didn't get that Shea and Jaz were so upset. Then Jaz directly asks Meghan if she knew anything.

:JAZ

Meghan admitted she'd seen them dancing and hadn't bothered to tell me. Yeah, she was a bitch, and how much do you think I cared? Um, okay, let's see. You find pictures of your boyfriend with some skanky girl, are you going to sit around and cry because your friend forgot to tell you? Or do you figure out your next move?

•

:MEGHAN

The pictures made Jaz so jealous that she got back with Tyler that night. And like two days later discovered the other pics on his cell.

JAZ IS COOL WITH HER BOYFRIEND'S CASUAL ENCOUNTER AND FORGIVES HIS URGE FOR PHOTO DOCUMENTATION.

:SHEA

Jaz talked to Tyler about it. She was chill about it. They were cool. She knows it meant nothing to him. Jaz bounces back. The day after she found the pics on his cell we were hanging out at her pool, swimming. Doing our nails. The usual. Like nothing had happened, because she's like that.

:LINDSIE

Jaz called me in and showed me when she posted the pics. It was harsh, but what was I going to do, tell her to take them off?

She says she didn't mean for anyone to know they were of Tyler and Kristyn, but yeah right. Kristyn's face was completely visible even though it was somewhat distorted. So next thing it was like the Paris Hilton video and the pics were all over mydamnspace... and nothing is ever censored there... they have the grossest things on there... but then someone's sister saw it and someone told their parents.

 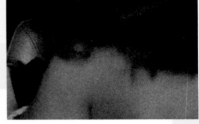

(Kristyn)

 :JAZ

THE PARENTS SPAZ OUT.

All the parents started trying to stalk us on mydamnspace. They were like you are so grounded and everyone had to go through this horrible week, the worst week ever. They were all: do you really do this, how come you have these sexual icons on here, how come you call each other biotches and hos? Oh my god, have you all been having sex with each other since you were five? Meghan's mother was like — do I have to take you to Planned Parenthood now? My father's still lecturing me about how I should only smoke marijuana on weekends — and I'm like God, do you think I smoke it every day before breakfast? And the pathetic thing is I barely ever get high, I don't even like it.

:SHEA

We were all like don't worry Mom, don't freak out, Dad, we're not like that, the other people are. Luckily they didn't ever see our pages. We were like it's all a joke, that's just how people talk, we're virgins, we would never smoke, we graduated from the Drugs Are Really Evil program, remember?

:LINDSIE

So we had to put up new mydamnspace pages under different names and say we were from other cities and zip codes so no one could track us down. It was a complete pain.

:SHEA

JAZ'S CURE FOR HANGOVERS AND MEGHAN'S FINAL DECISION.

But Jaz never gets all depressed for more than one hour. Even when she breaks up with Tyler. She's always like: what are we doing? Come on let's party, biatch. If you're like sick from partying the day before, she makes it into something fun. She even has this cure — she makes us run around the outside of our house four times and then chug a bottle of Diet Pepsi and she stays on the phone while you do it. It works, too.

:LINDSIE

She can get you to laugh like, snap! Stupid shit. Like this time we were eating Taco Bell and watching a Laguna rerun at Shea's and at the commercial Meghan started whining that something smelled bad and Jaz went into this whole snorting routine, sniffing around the bed. Is it garbage, she said, is it farts, is it — wait — it's Taco Bell! You had to be there. She's freakin' funny like that. She helped us survive the whole being grounded experience. When we were finally ungrounded, I was so freakin' happy to break out of the womb.

:SHEA

Today, at school, Jaz basically got in Meghan's face and said are you with me or not? There's this empty classroom we sneak into almost every day after lunch — we change our outfits, hang out, whatever. Things were really tense when we were hanging out there today. I would totally get if Jaz didn't want us to hang out with Meghan anymore, but Jaz is not like that. She puts on a harsh front sometimes but on the inside she is really the coolest, sweetest girl. Basically today she was like — Meghan are you with us, or aren't you?

:MEGHAN

Jaz confronted me in the hallway, all drama-drama, and I was of course like yeah, I'm not a backstabber, because I'm NOT.
And later we were all in the room and it was pretty awkward, but no one was directly saying anything about the situation. I wanted to talk about it so bad, but it seemed too dramatic. It's just not my nature to say fuck you and storm out or whatever.

:JAZ

Life is too short to have regrets. It was a frickin' joke, those pics. It got out of hand because a certain whore decided to make her own bad situation worse. What do you want me to say — Kristyn's a big whore, but she's my big whore, and I want her back? Actually I have no feelings for her at all. She's lucky, in a way. Some people would have kicked someone's booty. I'm not the violent type, violence makes me vomit, seriously. And Meghan can be friends with anyone she wants, I am so not into controlling. I just want everyone to chill. I just want my bitches to be happy, know what I'm sayin'?

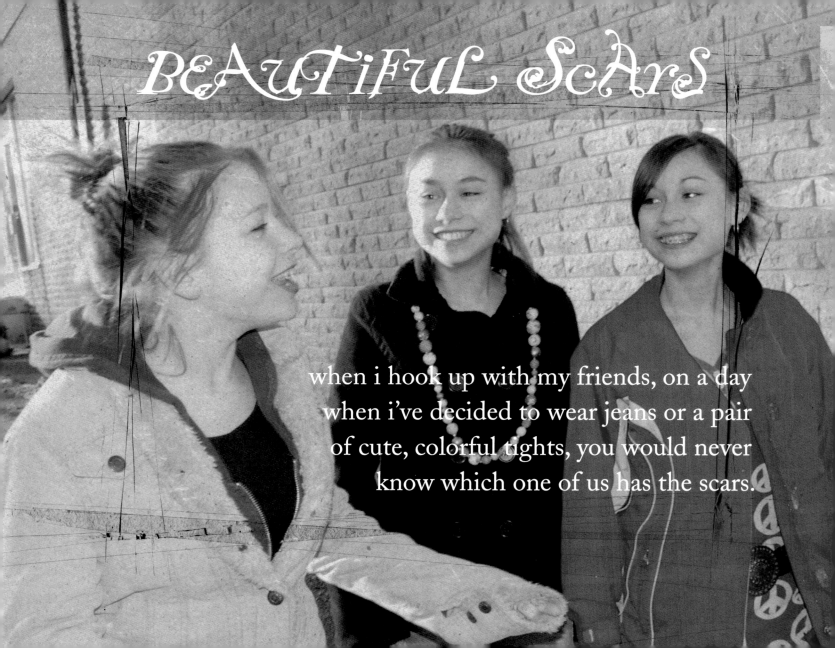

BEAUTIFUL SCARS

when i hook up with my friends, on a day
when i've decided to wear jeans or a pair
of cute, colorful tights, you would never
know which one of us has the scars.

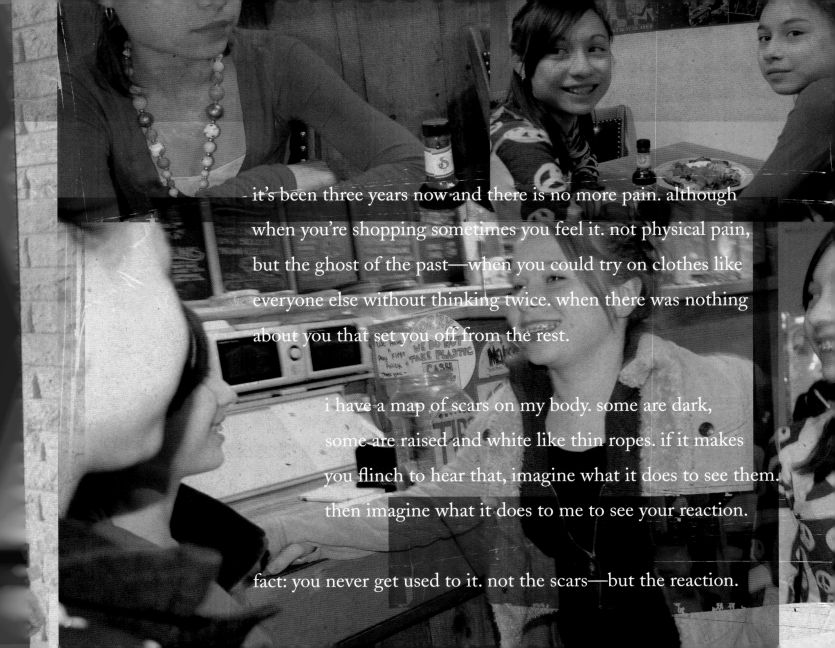

it's been three years now and there is no more pain. although when you're shopping sometimes you feel it. not physical pain, but the ghost of the past—when you could try on clothes like everyone else without thinking twice. when there was nothing about you that set you off from the rest.

i have a map of scars on my body. some are dark, some are raised and white like thin ropes. if it makes you flinch to hear that, imagine what it does to see them. then imagine what it does to me to see your reaction.

fact: you never get used to it. not the scars—but the reaction.

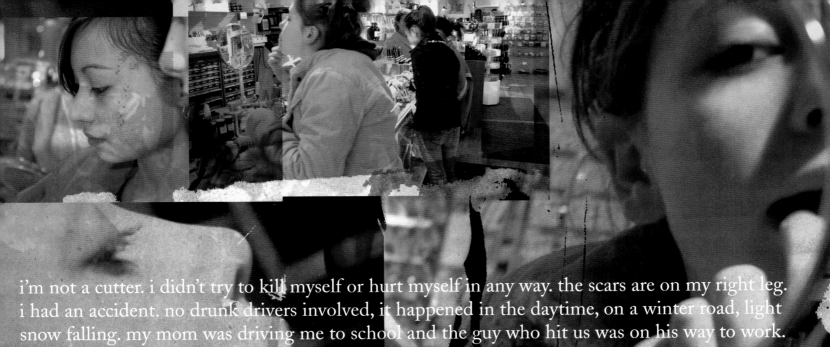

i'm not a cutter. i didn't try to kill myself or hurt myself in any way. the scars are on my right leg. i had an accident. no drunk drivers involved, it happened in the daytime, on a winter road, light snow falling. my mom was driving me to school and the guy who hit us was on his way to work. he was taking it nice and easy and when his car hit a patch of ice and went into a skid, time slowed. it took so long for him to hit us that it was almost like a ballet. my mom had time to say a short prayer out loud and i had time to be grateful that she said it.

the car was totaled. no one but me was hurt. i didn't think it was so bad at first. the shock covered the pain—for a while. halfway through the ambulance ride, the pain woke up and i'll spare you the details about the rest. i spent two days in the hospital in a haze of painkillers. no one wanted to tell me, but finally my father did: they were worried i might lose my leg.

i had four operations. six months of recovery. six more months of therapy. by the time i was walking, i wasn't thinking about scars. but some of my so-called friends were.

when something like this happens you really find out who your friends are. the real ones visit all the time, hold your hand, wipe your tears and keep telling you you're going to be okay. i basically have two best friends and i don't think i would have made it without them being there.

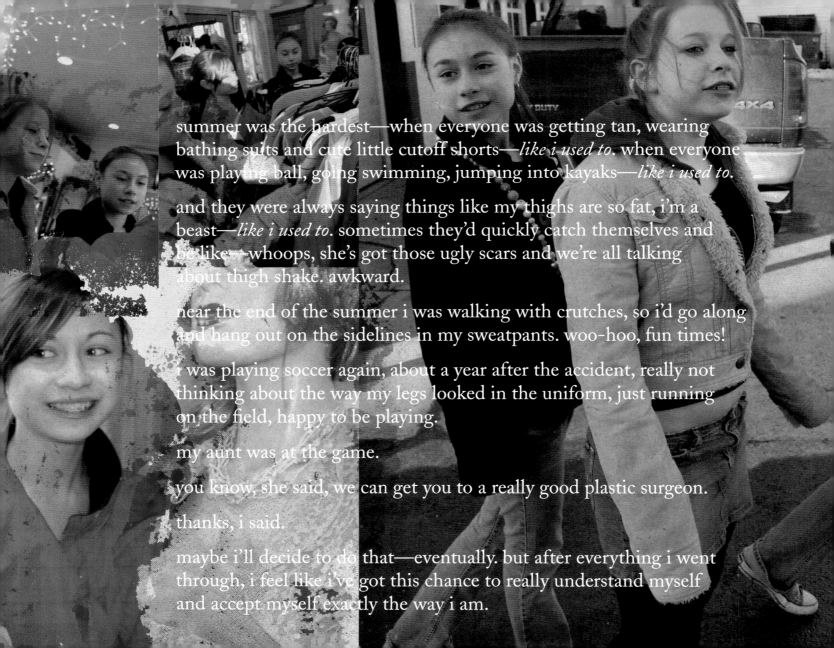

summer was the hardest—when everyone was getting tan, wearing bathing suits and cute little cutoff shorts—*like i used to*. when everyone was playing ball, going swimming, jumping into kayaks—*like i used to*.

and they were always saying things like my thighs are so fat, i'm a beast—*like i used to*. sometimes they'd quickly catch themselves and be like—whoops, she's got those ugly scars and we're all talking about thigh shake. awkward.

near the end of the summer i was walking with crutches, so i'd go along and hang out on the sidelines in my sweatpants. woo-hoo, fun times!

i was playing soccer again, about a year after the accident, really not thinking about the way my legs looked in the uniform, just running on the field, happy to be playing.

my aunt was at the game.

you know, she said, we can get you to a really good plastic surgeon.

thanks, i said.

maybe i'll decide to do that—eventually. but after everything i went through, i feel like i've got this chance to really understand myself and accept myself exactly the way i am.

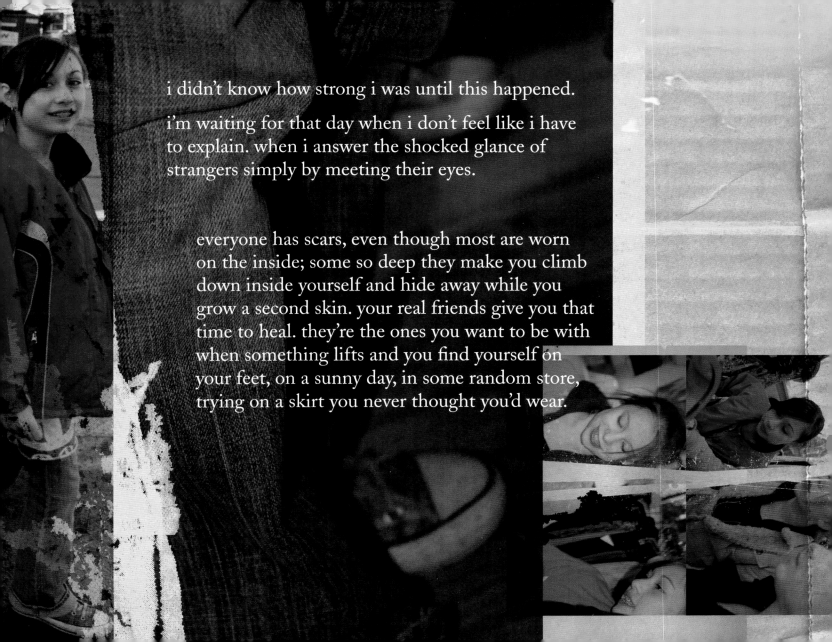

i didn't know how strong i was until this happened.

i'm waiting for that day when i don't feel like i have to explain. when i answer the shocked glance of strangers simply by meeting their eyes.

everyone has scars, even though most are worn on the inside; some so deep they make you climb down inside yourself and hide away while you grow a second skin. your real friends give you that time to heal. they're the ones you want to be with when something lifts and you find yourself on your feet, on a sunny day, in some random store, trying on a skirt you never thought you'd wear.

HOW TO FAIL SPANISH
(or at least the midterm)
En doce pasos fáciles[1]

[1] *in twelve easy steps*

Estimated Time
for Chapter:
11-12 hours

38

STEP ONE

Plan in advance! Three days before the test, begin begging your mom to unground you—long enough to let you study at your best friend's house! Convince her that a sleepover will maximize your studying time. Use reason, logic, and quiet determination: Her parents will make sure you stay on track, since they're reasonable people and it's a school night.

STEP TWO)

(Estimated time: 2 hours)

Score! Your bf's parents are out for the night. Celebrate this fact for an appropriate amount of time, choosing from any of these suggested activities: do your nails, tell your bf's little brother that he's a hermaphrodite, find out if it's true that you can use toothpaste to get rid of zits, explain in detail how Cody G. brushed past you in the hall and why it was not an accident, call Cody G. with the plan to hang up but only dial five of his digits, or if feeling particularly creative, lie on the floor and thoughtfully practice forging your mother's signature.

EW. →

Aunque eso es una acción criminal desaconsejable, duh.[2]

did u c zoe FREAK At lunch? No. y did she? i.d.k.

[2] *Although that's an inadvisable criminal action, duh.*

STEP THREE

(Estimated time: 2 minutes)

Seriously map out a viable studying strategy. **Sólo bromeando.[3]**

[3] *Just kidding.*

No you're not.

STEP FOUR 4+4+4 FOURRRRR

(Estimated time: 1 minute)

Seriously consider opening the Spanish book. **Sólo bromeando.**

STEP FIVE

(Estimated time: 30 minutes)

A key to success is judging your time wisely—but it's only eightish, so stop stressing!

The food of the gods.

Now's the time to consume massive amounts of energy food: king-size jalapeño Doritos (dipped in cool ranch dressing), Twix, Hot Tamales, fudge brownie low-fat yogurt pops, Sour Patch watermelon candies. Wash it down with some of that diet lime cola in the back of the fridge—boy her mom is cool.

¡Buen provecho![4] *¡AY DÍOS MÍO!*

While eating, be sure to watch *93 Beachouse Lane* because:

A. you need to find out if Crystal actually got the boob operation even though her twin sister didn't, and

B. you are studiously avoiding getting salsa stains on the Spanish book, although it might add an authentic culinary layer to the text. . . .

¡Pidan disculpa despuesde eructar, muchachas![5]

[4] *Enjoy your meal!*

[5] *Say "excuse me" after you burp, girls!*

mii cell went off in math.

LOL

not, they took iit!

Mr. McCart is HOT!

Caliente!

omg i wan sour p kids

the green onez taste linked

oop

40

STEP SIX
(Estimated time: 1 hour)

A study partner **can help** you avoid pitfalls you might not see.
Dude, says your pal, *is there multiple* choice *on chapters three and four or vocab words from the whole first section?*
Time to go online to get crucial notes from that geek, Regina Marsdale!

(Ella es básicamente una perdedora pero podría ser útil en esta situación.)[6]

Remember (whoopsie) that Regina Marsdale never goes online. But as long as you're online, hone your abstract thinking abilities by building a virtual boyfriend on yourperfectdude.com. This could really come in handy when it's time to conjugate those verbs in español.

STEP SEVEN
(Estimated time: 45 minutes)

Okay, time to stop messing around. You cannot put it off another second. You've been reckless with your time and if you don't do it now, it will definitely be too late, because the pizza place stops delivering at ten P.M., so make that call!

No te rompa la uña.[7]

[6] *(She is basically a loser but could be useful in this situation.)*

[7] *Don't break your fingernail.*

(Estimated time: 1-2 hours)

You've eaten, you've had your fun, now consider tripling your study power with the scientifically proven ability of music to enhance the rote memorization process.

La musica es chevere.[8]

[8] *Music is cool.*

Go ahead, throw on the damn music channel! Eminem should do it. *Basta!* NO, NO—not that lame song "Square Dance"! "Square Dance" sucks and you suck if you think it doesn't!

Tu chupas! Ella chupar. Que todo nos chupar.[9]

[9] *You suck! She sucks. We all suck.*

This isn't helping anyone's brain. Kindly regroup and indulge in a constructive argument about the merits of Bright Eyes. One of you says yes, one says no. Girls, this will not do! Think of the big picture, think of joyful interaction, blissful cooperation. Think, as a third alternative, of . . . My Chemical Romance. That's the way! See how much you can accomplish with a compromise? Now why not dance a bit? Why not dance a lot?

Bailen, muchachas, bailen.[10]

[10] *Dance, girls, dance.*

STEP NINE

(Estimated time: 1 minute)

Check the clock. It's two A.M. The test is in less than six hours.

Pero no te preocupes—¡ocho horas es un tiempo muy largo![11]

[11] *But don't spaz—eight hours is a long time!*

STEP TEN

(Estimated time: speed of light)

Hurry! Clear away all incriminating evidence and be at the table with your books, paper, and pens—the parents have arrived! Look at them with pale, scholarly faces. Ask them how their evening was. Give off faint glows of appreciation when they compliment you on your studiousness. When they suggest that you have studied long enough and should probably head to bed, trudge off gratefully, like sleep is what you need and crave. Then sneak out because what you're actually craving is food. Only two things left in the fridge: some old cheese and Dad's chocolate donuts he's saving to take to work. Do not touch the donuts! And the cheese

has blue hairy stuff on it! Gross, that is so disgusting! Doesn't anyone know how to stock a fridge? You want to puke! Now laugh so hard that you practically wet your pants! Crawl back to the bedroom. Good job, girls, well done!

43

STEP ELEVEN

(Estimated time: 3 hours)

The sky is growing light—it's so cool and eerie, life is so mysterious and beautiful, lack of sleep is so energizing and—hey—the test!

Panic forces you to take out the books once more. Silly girls! Don't you realize that the sleep deprivation chemicals are about to fully kick in (**¿No sera un alivio?**)[12] and you will soon be so manic and giddy that you will be good only for making lists of boys you have kissed, girls who are lame, and things you plan to do some day—like move to Brazil and be a famous Brazilian basketball player. Or a pimp! No, pimps are jerks. They're guys, anyway. They're guys and they're jerks. So Brazil. Basketball. Do they have chocolate donuts there, you really want a chocolate donut. Wait, what language do they speak there? Look this up on the Internet. Decide immediately to learn Portuguese. Or at least sneak back into the kitchen and get a donut. Who cares about Dad and his donuts! Why take one, eat them all!

Necesitará la energía para esa prueba.[13]

[12] *(Won't that be a relief?)*

[13] *You'll need energy for that test.*

STEP TWELVE

Are those birds chirping — or OMG! It's the fake bird alarm clock, and it's time to grab those books—luckily you slept on them, so hopefully the words seeped into your brain during that one hour of shut-eye! An extra bonus: You're still in your clothes from the night before, so no time wasted getting dressed! You're out the door—groggy but hopeful. And after all that careful studying, if you think you're going to ace the test—**usted esta completamente soñando!**[14]

¹⁴ *You are completely dreaming!*

On the bus, you'll probably want to keep your grades up by outlining an extra credit project—involving extensive teamwork. Long, hard hours. Intensive concentration. *¡Aye Dios Mio!*

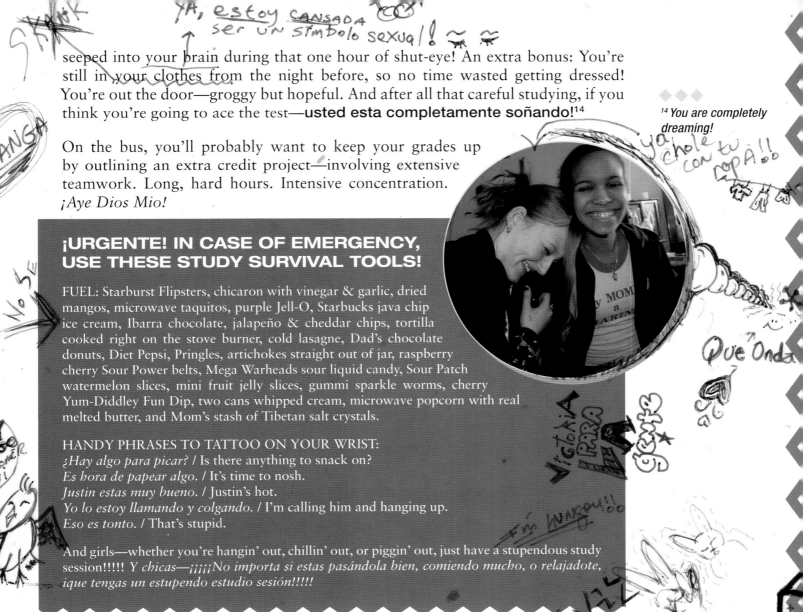

¡URGENTE! IN CASE OF EMERGENCY, USE THESE STUDY SURVIVAL TOOLS!

FUEL: Starburst Flipsters, chicaron with vinegar & garlic, dried mangos, microwave taquitos, purple Jell-O, Starbucks java chip ice cream, Ibarra chocolate, jalapeño & cheddar chips, tortilla cooked right on the stove burner, cold lasagne, Dad's chocolate donuts, Diet Pepsi, Pringles, artichokes straight out of jar, raspberry cherry Sour Power belts, Mega Warheads sour liquid candy, Sour Patch watermelon slices, mini fruit jelly slices, gummi sparkle worms, cherry Yum-Diddley Fun Dip, two cans whipped cream, microwave popcorn with real melted butter, and Mom's stash of Tibetan salt crystals.

HANDY PHRASES TO TATTOO ON YOUR WRIST:
¿Hay algo para picar? / Is there anything to snack on?
Es hora de papear algo. / It's time to nosh.
Justin estas muy bueno. / Justin's hot.
Yo lo estoy llamando y colgando. / I'm calling him and hanging up.
Eso es tonto. / That's stupid.

And girls—whether you're hangin' out, chillin' out, or piggin' out, just have a stupendous study session!!!!! *Y chicas—¡¡¡¡¡No importa si estas pasándola bien, comiendo mucho, o relajadote, ¡que tengas un estupendo estudio sesión!!!!!*

DEAR DAD,

it's weird but the more of these letters i write — this is #4 — the more i feel like we have an actual relationship. i have this eerie sense that T H I S is the time you're really going to write back. even if it's a postcard, i def don't care! i know you're completely swamped as usual. i went through my entire day today trying to imagine what you were doing — while i was getting up you were probably just going to sleep, whatever, i sound like a stalker.

my birthday was pretty low-key, had my best — (my only?) — friend over, rented some dvds, mom got thai take-out. went hiking the next day.

who am i kidding!! i DON`T want to write another nice letter to you! my feelings are screaming inside my head and i need to get them out!

i'm a little pissed about the song, still, dad.

IN FACT I AM SO FUCKING
PISSED I KNOW i'm not going
to SEND YOU THIS LETTER

it'll be just ANOTHER ONE
IN MY fucking NOTEBOOK
THAT NEVER GETS
MAILED.

did it ever cross your mind to ANSWER
one of my letters instead of turning
them into a cheap moment in one
of your hit songs?

do you not REALIZE that
DEAR DAD is playing everywhere
in the gym where i work out, at the
school dances, it's a fucking ring tone
on half my friends' cells.

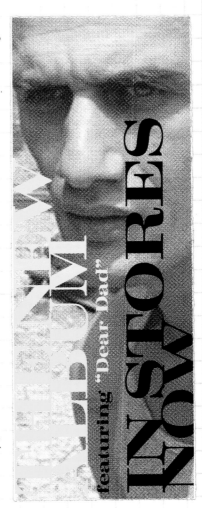

everyone keeps asking if it was about me and you. and i of course laugh it off. i never wrote him a letter in my fucking life, i say. we talk all the time on the phone! i don't tell them that you DID NOT EVEN CALL ON MY BIRTHDAY.

(But thanks for the case of Fiji, the buddhist flag and the $3,000 computer w. built-in web cam — even though i am NOT a buddhist don't drink Fiji (we have unpolluted water up here) and i STOPPED USING the computer TWO MONTHS ago BECAUSE OF YOU!!! I and i'm going to take that first hand written song of yours and i'm gonna sell it on eBay today!!!!!)

and WTF IS UP WITH THAT SHIT VIDEO for the DEAR DAD song, with you starring as THE BRAIN-DEAD ROCK STAR WHO CAN'T DEAL WITH HIS GUILT ABOUT HIS DAUGHTER SO HE SHOVES HER LETTERS IN A DRAWER AND JUST GOES AND DOES LINES WITH SOME WHORE IN A BACK ROOM!

How obvious and predictable!

and YTF does that girl in the pool in the video, YTF does she look like an ugly version of me, and my friend ava thinks so too. i mean you could have at least let me star in it, instead of that inferior clone! Dude, do you not ever think i might crave my 15 minutes of fame? Personally i think that would have been a brilliant birthday gift: we may have a shitty, pathetic relationship but hell, he let me star in my own video. JK, i do not want to be in a pathetic, phony video.

Will i tell you any of this? NO!!! because i am a loser coward loser.

i'm glad mom had the balls to move, it's ok here because there are a few normal stable people but otherwise I HATE IT HERE TOO, almost as much as hollywood!!!

reason one:

i can't escape you! everyone from my lame-ass math teacher to random bank tellers want to know if i could possibly introduce you to them when you come here, as if you'd ever come to this town and as if you'd spend your time meeting lame-ass bank tellers and math teachers, actually you probably would be nicer to them than me, as long as they were asking for your autograph.

reason two:

your songs are everywhere, your posters are everywhere, but YOU are nowhere. it hurts when i'm at a school concert and everyone else's dad is there. it hurts when i eat at a friend's house and her dad is at the table making jokes or asking how she's doing at school or even giving her a hard time. at least he is THERE. WHERE ARE YOU?

reason three:

all that fake shit and pressure and social status crap exists here too!

what's the difference if it's paris fUCKING hilton who's looking me up and down and wondering if i'm somebody, or kaitlin fUCKING langley, a random ditz from my tenth grade class, wondering if i'm good enough to ask to her party until she finds out i'm your daughter and then of course i'm in.

WTF is wrong with everyone? how did the world get this way? it's like someone decided that people should act phony, snotty, bitchy, shallow and slutty and if you don't fit into one of those roles, then you will have NO IDENTITY AT ALL!

and i am just as bad, no one knows what really goes on inside me. i don't act perfect, but i only let out my crazy side and my real feelings when i'm partying — like everyone else.

So i am "popular." i don't give a fuck, but it's better than being a freakish loner. you have to have somewhere to go on weekends. people think i'm "so nice". I'M NOT!

AND i will NEVER tell THEM or YOU what i really feel.

like how much i miss you and how i never forget how it was when i was little, stupid moments i wish would just leave my head, like the time i got up and you were sitting in front of the TV watching cartoons and you were in such a good mood and we watched them for hours and ate donuts. it's such a pathetic shabby memory but i was happy back then.

do you even remember those times? do you even care who i am now? i want to send you some new pics, dad, but do you even look at them? are you going to turn them into a song, or just drop them straight into the garbage?

here's one from when i went hiking with my friend ava. can you tell i hate the cold up here and miss the L.A. sun even though it's full of smog, just like i miss you and your warmth even though it's polluted and poisoned?

you don't know anything about me.

i wish you would call me up once and just ask, like you really wanted to know, what i was doing, not just "dude, what's up!" and then start talking about yourself and how busy you are.

i want you to care. i want you to be proud of me.

i literally stopped using the computer because of what you said. i'm such a loser remembering every fucking word you say, like one of your loser fans.

but that time we were walking by the santa monica pier last summer — you said that evil beauty spills out onto the page when you use ink instead of a computer. DO YOU EVEN REMEMBER?

i've been writing so much and i'm trying to get the nerve to send you something. like this screenplay. i've written the first ten pages over so many times. it's also called dear dad. i have this dream it could be a real movie and that you'll really get it and maybe even star in it. i keep imagining you could do the soundtrack. we could work on it together, like that time in the recording studio on la cienega. that was so much fucking fun. do you think we could ever do that? do you think it's any good?

was i insane thinking about selling your first song? that is my most perfect possession. i love the drawings in the margins, i love the lyrics.

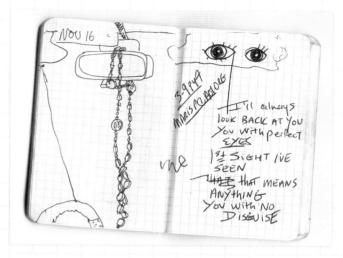

i wish you still wrote songs like that, not about some loser dad who doesn't write his daughter back. or forget about songs — i wish you'd just write to me!

when we said goodbye at the airport — five months ago, i haven't even SEEN you since and only talked to you three times, dad — but you gave me that envelope and i thought, big deal it's money, or maybe even a joint. but when i saw it was the FiRSt SONG YOU EVER WROTE ... "WiTH NO DiSGUiSE." i was like crying on the plane. i felt like you were telling me that you still loved me like You did when i was a baby.

it was such a pure song, and i didn't think it was corny at all, the whole idea of looking into a baby's eyes and seeing them looking back at you with no disguise. it was like you could just see the father had no disguise either, all the bullshit and phoniness of the world just disintegrated in that one moment, in that one beautiful idea.

i'm proud of you dad, obviously, you were my hero and
always will be.

but i want you to feel the same way about me.

while i'm sitting here at the kitchen counter, writing
you this insane letter that will never be mailed, i keep
looking up at the picture of you on the fridge. the one
i took in Marin county, you sitting on that $80,000
custom Harley or whatever. remember?????

and while i'm looking at this picture of you, i keep thinking —

are you somewhere looking back?

i'm going to write you a real letter now. i want to tell you everything that's going on in my heart but that's so hard to do when you don't know if the person is going to hate you for saying it.

the one true thing i'll tell you is —
    i love you.
    and dad — this time i need you to answer.

got back
REBUTTAL from a girl with curves

wut it do, ma girlz, wut it do?
u hit ^ da page so must b u cravin $um info.

fact 1:
back when i waz lil, i waz takin dance cla$$e$ with girlz like chelsealaurenalexakelli &
they all lookin at me with they $tank ho faces like what iz d@ THANG & i waz 4 real
thinking-- how ime $poze 2 focu$ on ma routine wit $um anorexic- a$$ bootayz in ma face &
not even known how 2 $hake they laffytaffy bcuz how u can $hake wut u ain't got?
they all thinkin they da $hyt. word: hair bleach, small bonze & a manic metabolizm do not
make you da $hyt. feel me on d@.

so i waz hatin 2. hmmmmmmm.

fact 2:
i <33 my body. n/e/thing u got urself born wit iz g%d unless you trine 2 fit in wit da
wrong crowd. feel me on d@.

think about it: i could have MAN HANDS, now there iz a gurl i hang wit who haz herself
some MAN HANDS & what is she goin 2 do wit her MAN HANDS, get reductive surgury? sit on
that shyt?

& what about freakin head shapes? like dis 1 girl leandra, she posesses a strange-ass
hed shape--one of those flat backhed people, they say they mamas never turned them when
they waz in the crib. so wat she gonna do, chop her damn hed off? u could hide under
a hat but then your hed would eventually prolly go bald.

so u got sum big-ass nostrils, sum dubble chin axshunn, sum stump-ugly toes, wtf? are you spoze 2 peel yer whole self off & then what about yer intestinal parts? u can't exactly dress d@ mess up & take it out shopping 4 shoes.

i hung out in my womb meditating on d@ situation.

what iz an a$$ & y iz it such a big-a$$ed deal? they $hould chalk that $hyt on a $koo black board an make u think about it. if they hit us ^ wit sum practical facts, like flat a$$, phat a$$, u got 2 let that concept go.

yeh, i bounced back from a lil bitta nuthin.

fact 3: u gotta mix it ^.
my new crew iz crackin. we are not r asses, we r not r colors, we r not da clothes. itz da mix d@ makes it pop, so no more trine 2 hate on me, coz i'll keep on havin a variety of facets. girlz u know u got 2 mind ur own diamond & shine on, shine!

jus showin yall sum love. scream @ cha gurl again when u getta chance.holla.

The Red Dress

6 a.m.

got up.

i wore the red dress.

the entire day sucked from that point on.

there were only two good things about the day.

ben.

and the school nurse.

this is what happened.

went to the rehearsal of the molière play and ben and me had the wrong day,
they were still building the set.
teachers bitched at me about the dress.

someone called me a ho. some girls said if i didn't want to be
stared at why didn't i wear normal clothes. i had a breakdown
and just sat on the floor of the hall, kids streaming around me.

ben didn't know what to do. someone
asked me was i on drugs or sick or
what. i said i was sick to get out of gym.
so we went to the nurse's office.

ben came with me.

the nurse was cool. i thought she was going to say something about my dress

but she said, wow, it's glamorous, don't you kids say glam,
is that what you call it nowadays.
she said we could just sit on the cots—
but not on the same one.

i sat there and thought about how i was in prison.

that's when i realized that the day was perfect. that only the people in it made it bad.

i imagined the entire day happening without one other person in the whole school. except ben and the nurse. seriously, empty halls, the light all green and like an aquarium, no people to impress, no rules, school would be perfect. and then the bell rang

and i ran the hell out of there. do you ever do that, not even think? just get up and go?

i kept running.

but the halls are a rat maze and they carry you in circles. so i ran into ben.

he said, everyone's gone,
let's wander around the place.
even though he was basically
reading my mind, it didn't
sound fun anymore.

i'm out of here, i said. you do
what you want.

but we decided to go to the gym anyway—and we messed around because everyone had gone home for real.

i said, hey ben, i bet you didn't know that i know how to fly.

yeah, right, he said. did that nurse give you drugs?

for real, i said, watch. and then i jumped off
this ledge thingie, not really high.

but ben looked surprised. your dress is like a parachute he said.
he says things like that.

so at least there were two people today who got the red dress.

Ms. Delgado
Photography Final

Assignment:

**Choose a human subject and create a project in Photoshop
consisting of at least thirty photographs, text where necessary.
At least ten pages, to be presented in one of the following forms:
graphic novel, photojournalist article, or a mixture of your own
making. Your project MUST contain the following:**

1. A visual introduction of yourself (set your camera on auto-shoot and
timer) and a statement about your intention of purpose and why you
chose your subject.

2. Shots of the subject in at least three different locations (school, work,
party, etc.).

3. Shots of the subject with friends (at least one, but the more the
merrier). This shot should convey emotion and interaction.

4. Shots of one of your subject's family members.

5. Shots of the subject engaged in something they are passionate
about.

6. Shots of inanimate objects belonging to the subject. (These should
convey something about the subject.)

7. At least one full-page photograph.

Remember—this will be your ONLY graded project this year, and you will
(hopefully) be using everything we learned. Your project will be graded
on merit of individual photos, how well you demonstrate knowledge of
Photoshop, and overall originality of approach. HAVE FUN!!!!!!!

Mitra

by kasey

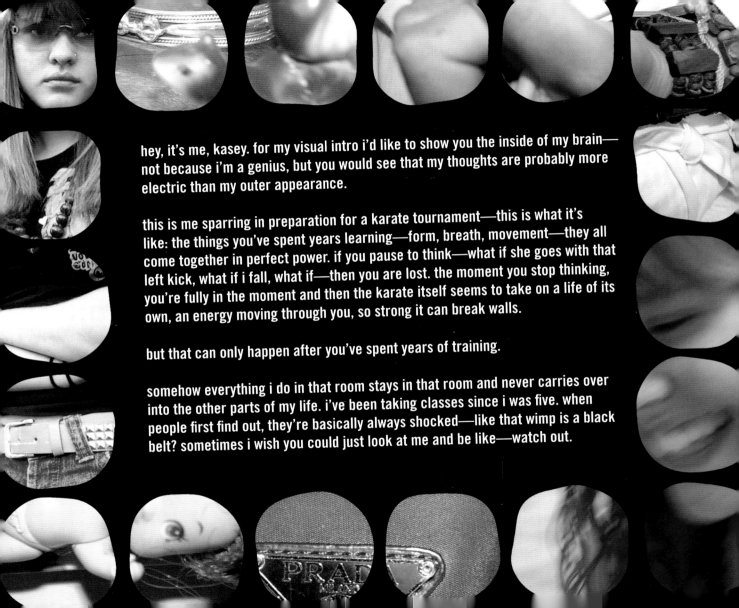

hey, it's me, kasey. for my visual intro i'd like to show you the inside of my brain—not because i'm a genius, but you would see that my thoughts are probably more electric than my outer appearance.

this is me sparring in preparation for a karate tournament—this is what it's like: the things you've spent years learning—form, breath, movement—they all come together in perfect power. if you pause to think—what if she goes with that left kick, what if i fall, what if—then you are lost. the moment you stop thinking, you're fully in the moment and then the karate itself seems to take on a life of its own, an energy moving through you, so strong it can break walls.

but that can only happen after you've spent years of training.

somehow everything i do in that room stays in that room and never carries over into the other parts of my life. i've been taking classes since i was five. when people first find out, they're basically always shocked—like that wimp is a black belt? sometimes i wish you could just look at me and be like—watch out.

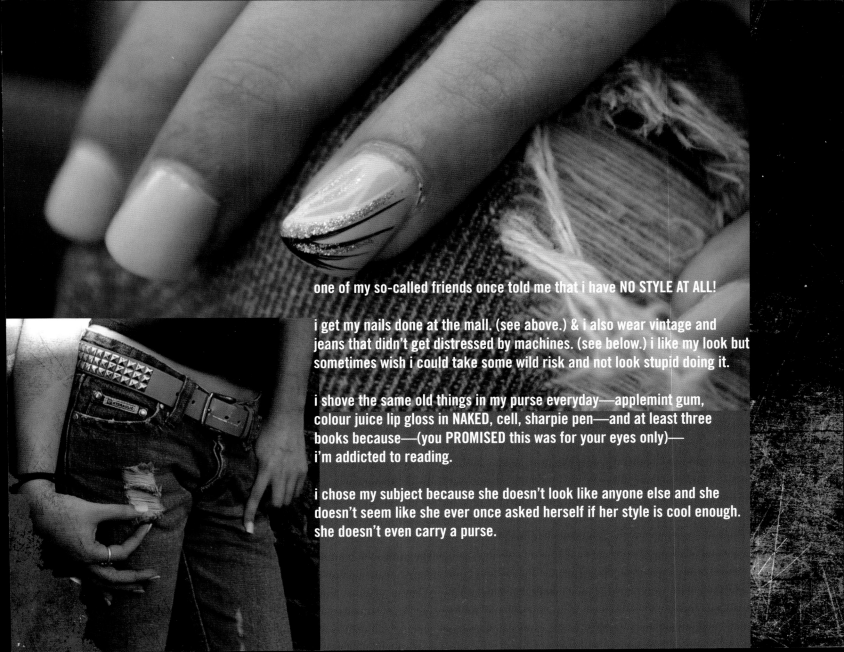

one of my so-called friends once told me that i have NO STYLE AT ALL!

i get my nails done at the mall. (see above.) & i also wear vintage and jeans that didn't get distressed by machines. (see below.) i like my look but sometimes wish i could take some wild risk and not look stupid doing it.

i shove the same old things in my purse everyday—applemint gum, colour juice lip gloss in NAKED, cell, sharpie pen—and at least three books because—(you PROMISED this was for your eyes only)— i'm addicted to reading.

i chose my subject because she doesn't look like anyone else and she doesn't seem like she ever once asked herself if her style is cool enough. she doesn't even carry a purse.

all anyone talks about at school is who's a loser, who's a freak, who's gay, who's bi, who's a punk, who thinks they're cool because they shop at hot topic, who's preppie, who's a stoner, who's an **IT GIRL**, who's a wannabe, who's a scene kid and who's trying to be something they're not, or who doesn't even **REALIZE** that they are what they say they're not.

nitro

doesn't fit any of the categories. i wanted to see how she really lived and figure her out. (she's in **THIS** class, but i never even talked to her before.)

when i saw her sitting on the street Saturday, i thought here's my chance, but all i DID was spastically snap her pic—and instead of talking to her, i walked away. thinking: i am so lame. the picture's a little stiff, and i was too shy to get as close with the camera as i wanted.

i go to the mall looking for safer subjects, but mitra keeps coming up in my mind. i get up my courage and gave her a call. she says when do you want to start. i say right now.

meet her in a coffee shop downtown with her best friend, jake.
topic a: mitra's mom found a mouse skull in the downstairs closet and it was SO disgusting that mitra can hardly talk about it but Jake wants to know if she kept it. why, do you want to make a necklace out of it, says mitra. ya never know, says jake.
mitra keeps refilling her coffee cup and adding 98 packets of sugar each time. she talks fast! her perfume smells like the beach— all coconut and oceany.

topic b: who's playing at slam-slam tomorrow at open mike. mitra's brother has a band and he's thinking about shaving his head before the gig. are you going? mitra asks me. um, maybe, i say. i do not tell her that my mother thinks only loser stoners go there. you should, she says. crow's band is so hot. crow is her brother?! cool, i say. i do not tell her that all my friends are crushing on her brother. i definitely do not say that i am never allowed out on school nights.

she draws this on daily.
you draw on your eye every day too, she says.
weird, but i never thought of eyeliner as drawing on my eye.

next morning.

mitra works every sunday afternoon at the community crisis center.
since it's dead she works on her project, does filing, and starts rummaging
through her bag for a scrap she was going to sew on her jacket.

this is her jacket.

bottle caps. heart she made. stuff she sewed on.
on her back, there's a vintage album cover that
she scanned into Photoshop and printed out
on iron-on material.

i get this idea.
i ask her to dump out her backpack so i can shoot the contents.
she doesn't even hesitate, it's so weird, she's calm about
everything. like, she doesn't even care that she has a tie-dye
t-shirt in there. she doesn't explain anything. how does she do that?

sketchbook, french homework, postcard from london, a cool book,
a rock she got from her last camping trip. even her normal things
make you want to steal them—ultra skinny purple ink pen, cell
phone with Japanese stickers on it. the stuff in her bag is so perfect
it's like she put it there ahead of time, but she didn't. i don't want to
stop there—i want to look in the pages of her sketchbook and read
the back of the postcard.

then crow comes.

oh you're one of them, he says when he sees me.

um, ok, i say.

i was just making up a theory about you guys at lunch, he says. at school, yesterday.

what are you talking about, i say.

yeah, who are you talking about, says mitra.

those girls, those ones who all look alike, the ones who fit into society, he says, i mean,

i was just thinking you're all living in a false reality. but maybe it's the opposite. maybe i am.

jesus, crow, mitra says, you can't just stereotype people. how do you even know who kasey is?

it's okay, i say quickly, he's right. i am ONE OF THEM.

forgive me, crow says, looking straight into my eyes. then he laughs. it's just life, though.

yeah, i say.

it's just something we all have to get through.

mitra seems annoyed by crow but she fake plays guitar with him anyway.

crow, she says, do you have any money—i'm craving a sweet potato burrito.

nada, he says. but i bet SHE does he says about me.

nada, i say. i don't tell him i have a credit card.

THEN THE CRISIS PHONE RINGS and i have to leave because everything's confidential.

wait in an outside office for forever until mitra opens the door again.

her eyes tell nothing.

how do you do it? i say. lame! too late to take back!

but she just looks at me. do what?

how do you handle those calls?

we get trained. you listen. you care. you tell them about practical things they can do.

i get pictures in my head of suicide attempts, hysterical, lonely people, hungry people.

i want to ask more, but she's back to pasting photos onto her project. have flash of jealousy—

it already looks cooler than mine. i'm watching how she works—it's not like she's planning it all out.

she just cuts a head off, draws a spontaneous black mark—and it's suddenly amazing.

and if i had the nerve to keep asking her
questions, what would I say—
how are you so brave?
how do you just jump right in and handle
whatever comes?

a bunch of their friends come by and
they help sort the donated clothes for the
homeless shelter. here, says mitra, try this
on. she hands me a small, red, low-cut shirt.
i don't say but isn't this for the homeless
people. i definitely don't say gosh, these
nasty clothes haven't been washed! for one
thing, the shirt is supercute, like a big-time
score in a vintage boutique.
shove the shirt in my backpack and make
them go outside to pose on the porch.
they're all pretty theatrical.

maybe you should use crow for my relative,
mitra says.
yeah, i got some okay shots i think.
but don't you want to see his show?
sure, i say.
and maybe you should come tomorrow and
shoot him at my house.
he might even shave his head, she says.
that would be supercool, i say.

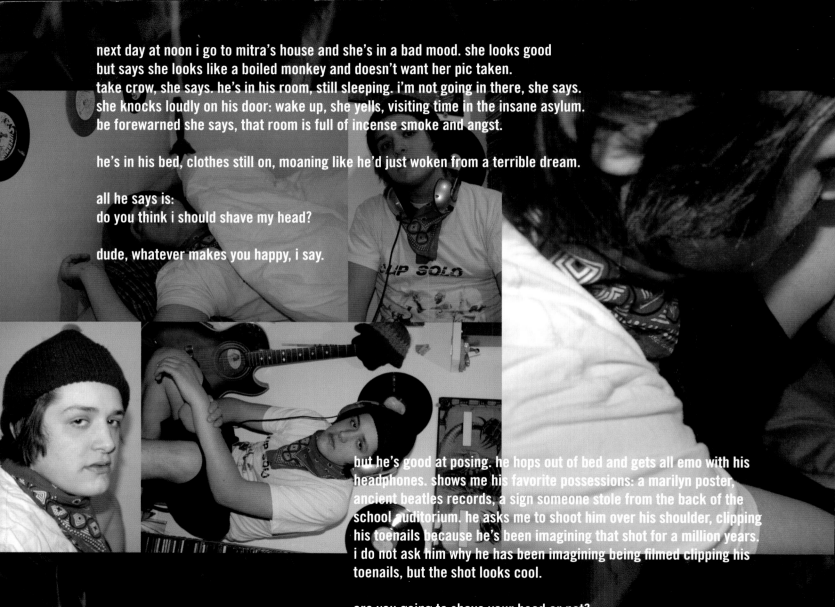

next day at noon i go to mitra's house and she's in a bad mood. she looks good
but says she looks like a boiled monkey and doesn't want her pic taken.
take crow, she says. he's in his room, still sleeping. i'm not going in there, she says.
she knocks loudly on his door: wake up, she yells, visiting time in the insane asylum.
be forewarned she says, that room is full of incense smoke and angst.

he's in his bed, clothes still on, moaning like he'd just woken from a terrible dream.

all he says is:
do you think i should shave my head?

dude, whatever makes you happy, i say.

but he's good at posing. he hops out of bed and gets all emo with his
headphones. shows me his favorite possessions: a marilyn poster,
ancient beatles records, a sign someone stole from the back of the
school auditorium. he asks me to shoot him over his shoulder, clipping
his toenails because he's been imagining that shot for a million years.
i do not ask him why he has been imagining being filmed clipping his
toenails, but the shot looks cool.

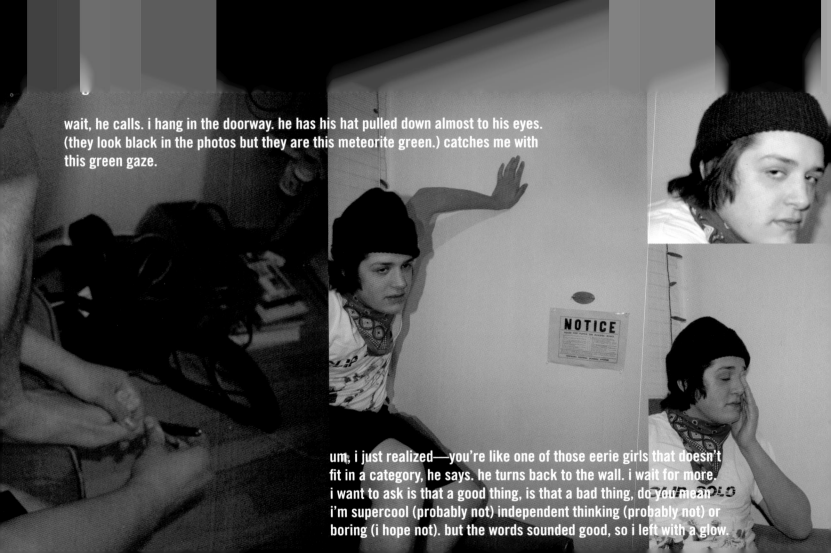

wait, he calls. i hang in the doorway. he has his hat pulled down almost to his eyes. (they look black in the photos but they are this meteorite green.) catches me with this green gaze.

um, i just realized—you're like one of those eerie girls that doesn't fit in a category, he says. he turns back to the wall. i wait for more. i want to ask is that a good thing, is that a bad thing, do you mean i'm supercool (probably not) independent thinking (probably not) or boring (i hope not). but the words sounded good, so i left with a glow.

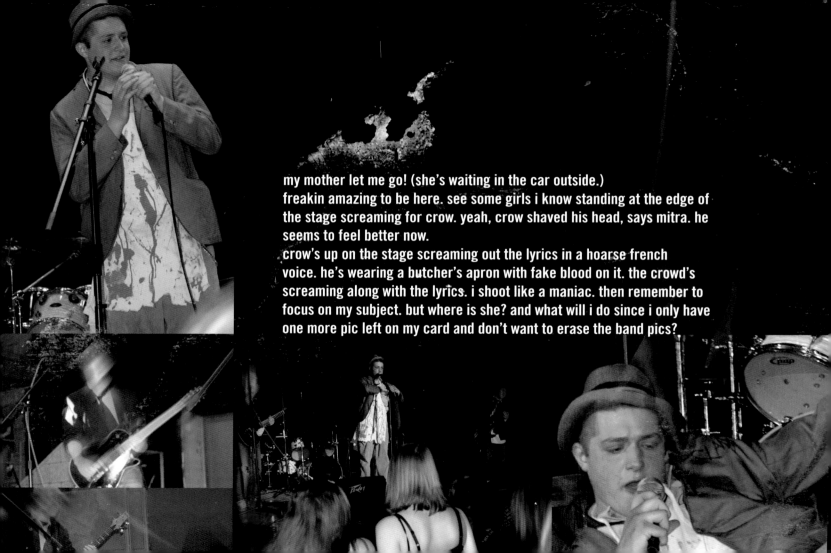

my mother let me go! (she's waiting in the car outside.)
freakin amazing to be here. see some girls i know standing at the edge of the stage screaming for crow. yeah, crow shaved his head, says mitra. he seems to feel better now.
crow's up on the stage screaming out the lyrics in a hoarse french voice. he's wearing a butcher's apron with fake blood on it. the crowd's screaming along with the lyrics. i shoot like a maniac. then remember to focus on my subject. but where is she? and what will i do since i only have one more pic left on my card and don't want to erase the band pics?

i find her in the crowd, doing a manic spinning
dance that perfectly captures her essence.
i feel a craving to get this shot more than any
so far— it's this gut thing—not like oh wouldn't
this shot be so interesting—it's more like: *i have
to have it because this is the one that is HER.*
only i'm too scared to move in and get it.
she's up close to the stage in a knot of her
friends. she's been nice to me until now, but
hello, she's my subject, not my friend and i don't
want her to hate me for invading her space with
my camera while she's all dancing and free.

but i want need have to have that shot.
and i've got this one shot left on the card.
do i jump in and grab it?
there's always a delay with digital.
what if i shoot and get just her nostrils or her
elbow? yeah i can erase that shot and try again,
but then the moment will be over.
suddenly i need to capture her spontaneity so
badly that adrenaline takes over the fear and
i remember everything i learned this year—
get in close, take a breath, let the camera see
for you—imagine your best shot—take a leap—
hope for the best—

How it is now

1.

I USED TO SHOP—
that baby phat jacket of mine
so red it burned a hole in the night.

(i didn't imagine
your existence.)

2.

I USED TO COME HOME LATE,
slipping in like
a vapor, to a bed
i couldn't feel beneath me.

(now your cries
interrupt
the shape of my dreams.
i fold you in
with me,
stay awake
to watch you sleep.)

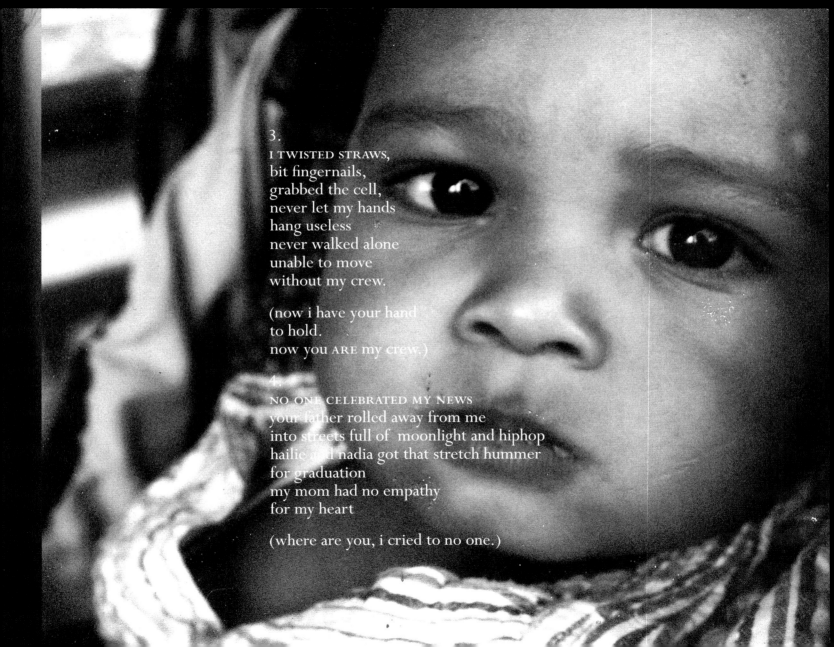

3.

I TWISTED STRAWS,
bit fingernails,
grabbed the cell,
never let my hands
hang useless
never walked alone
unable to move
without my crew.

(now i have your hand
to hold.
now you ARE my crew.)

4.

NO ONE CELEBRATED MY NEWS
your father rolled away from me
into streets full of moonlight and hiphop
hailie and nadia got that stretch hummer
for graduation
my mom had no empathy
for my heart

(where are you, i cried to no one.)

5.

I HID IN SOME BIG UGLY DRESSES,
what you'd wear on death row.
counted and figured and argued with
the months like i could get more than nine
i dreaded getting to the end
i went through it alone.

(i didn't realize you
were already with me.)

6.

I WOKE SLICK WITH TERROR
caught my strange self in the mirror
began to bare my stomach proudly
ignored the stares that said
put that thing away
i grew bigger

(at first flutters, then
one kick, then two
and i got it:
we were in this together.)

7.

YOU WORE BORN NAKED
no one celebrated but us
i held you and
your weight was sweet
i breathed in your innocence
i looked at you
to see what you were made of
and when you looked back
there were no questions in your eyes
there was nothing bad in your eyes

8.

I COULD SEE THAT THERE WERE THINGS
you would need
things i would hurry up
and have to be
things i had already started
to leave behind

9.

THAT BABY PHAT JACKET
so red it burned a hole in the night
a hole you were born through,
a jacket exchanged
for a stroller
to roll us
into *now*

dear it girl,

i am the girl who you think does not have feelings, because my face has learned not to show you.

i am the girl who you have called beast, freak, pig, psycho, lesbo, gross, pathetic, scary, retard—either secretly or not.

i am the girl who sits alone in the cafeteria, reading or fixed on my food. your chatter breaks over me like waves.

i'm the girl whose body will not do what i want it to. i'm the girl who mumbles if you speak to me. i don't know how to make small talk or say things to make you laugh. my mouth won't make a smile.

i'm the girl who has been shut out because of my weight or my race or the style of my hair, because i say weird things, because of the look on my face, because my timing is always off, because the shapes of my body parts are too big, long, flat, wide or different.

i'm the girl you hate for staring too long or never making eye contact. you think of me as hostile, but i'm so shy, i'm terrified.

i'm the girl who does nothing with her face. (because make-up makes me feel like a clown.)

i'm the girl who goes around with a hat on or my hair in my face. sometimes i keep my coat on, even on hot days. i hide in invisibly colored, baggy clothes, because the less you see of me the safer i feel. (except for that time

i showed up in the clothes i cut and painted myself, when you said i looked
like a loser; believe it or not i was trying for a style, only you didn't get it,
nobody did.)

i am the girl you know as—the one who has the weird brother, the one who
works at the CVS store, the one who always wears those tacky shoes, the
one who cried that time in gym in the fifth grade, the one who has that ugly
mark on her neck, the one rumored to have had sex at age nine. (not true.)

on the morning of every school day, i am the girl who puts on my mask
before leaving the house, even though it won't protect me.

i am the girl who wishes for one real friend.
you don't need to see my picture because you know who i am.

ALY
SWEET SIXTEEN

mardi gras masquerade

FEBRUARY 24
[EIGHT O'CLOCK]
LA FÉE VERTE

R. S. V. P.

welcome to my life.
whoever you are.

think of this scrapbook as the
uncensored version of what
REALLY HAPPENED on
the day the entire world
(minus one person)
came out to show me love
on what was supposed to be
the biggest night of my life.

aly's place

THESE ARE ME:
❖ PROFILE ❖
❖ BLOG
❖ PICS / VIDS
❖ FRIENDS
❖ ENEMIES
❖ MESSAGES

"somewhere over the"

[more photos]

female, 16 years
livingdeadtown, USA

currently online

hey, i'm Aly.
about me:
1. these are my sisters and i would die for them we've been through
everything people hate on us b/c they're jealous and they should be.

2. we're f-ing cheerleaders and unless you are one, you
don't know what that means. go to the nationals and you'll
see the reality of the situation — girls tumble, split
their heads open, blood runs on the floor. you have to be
strong, you have to love competition, you are an athlete —
and you work hard all year for it. the pay-off is just as
real. if you get that, you get me.

3. music, morning until night, birth until death. NEVER
SHUT IT OFF! Nano is god. sweet&sour Twizzlers come next.

(Tiffany, me, Keira)

4. i hate whiners. and narcissistic psychopaths. i love liars and phony people. J

5. people i want to hurt: the ones who say i hate labels — i'm a unique
individual! (you're probably a latent goth bitch & look just like your
mother!) And the ones who say: I HATE MYSPACE SLANG AND ABBREVIATIONS.
so spell it out all the way lame-ass, & shut up about it!!!!

6. yeah i am spoiled and i LOVE it. and I LOVE MY life.

Morning of my sixteenth fucking birthday. Morning *after* partying. (Celebrating in advance.) Only nine hours until my sweet sixteen. (If you're not in the pics, you know why):

A lot to do. Things go faster wit music.

I'm obsessed with that song, by 444, this new Weezerish group. Can you hear it blasting?

Whoever you are, I know you are there.
Wherever you are, I know you can feel me.
I know you can feel all the things going through me.

10 a.m.

We are so pumped about tonight. We will be. Even after all that shady ghetto spiced rum last night. Starbucks, where are you?

Don't get all emo, Kiera says. It's your b-day, baby! They drown out my song singing "Happy Birthday" in their hungover, off-key frog voices—shut them up quick.

how long will this song stay lasered into my mind? you have your first guy, and he's just the first. maybe you stay with him all through high school, but probably you don't. and then. and then— there's the second. you're more careful about the second because after that there's the THIRD. and then you're heading into slut territory. so unfair, THEY can do what they want but WE are on stage, constantly judged. i totally fucking wasted my second with HIM.

10:30 a.m.

These guys r deep in convo. About last night.
Who *cares* that Tyler's back with Jaz.
Who *cares* that Shawn didn't show at that ghetto club.
Come on, get movin', wish me happy b-day, r u going
to wear that rag to my party and if so maybe you should
put a thong on first.

Know what I wanted? I wanted you.
I get what I want. I always do.
When I don't want you anymore you'll know we're through.

Tiffany: Yeh, you're so gonna party tonight, so you better get undepressed.
Kiera: Who is that?
Tiff: It's Bo.
Kiera: What's wrong with him.
Tiff: Won't say. *(to him)* You did?
Kiera: He did what?
Tiff: Some girl. *(to him)* Duh, who? *(to us)* Some girl named Caitlin.
Kiera: Caitlin who? Caitlin Meudio or Caitlin Johnson?
Me: I really don't care. Hang up. Just tell him he's not gonna bring some ho to my party.
Tiff: *(to us)* He doesn't know her.
Kiera: Dude, he doesn't know her?
Tiff: Yeah, he doesn't know her last name.
Kiera: Gross, he could get AIDS from her.
Tiff: He says he's not even sure her first name is Caitlin.
Me: Tell him to wash his hands at least, before he comes tonight, he is *such* a slut.
Tiff: Comes tonight?
Me: Um, I'm gonna ignore that.

getting dressed, tried to push him
out of my mind, didn't want to
let him ruin my perfect day—
but kept flashing on the way he
pulled me in, the way he
looked at me, all the plans we
made for tonight, my friends
knew not to talk about it, but
they didn't know what kept
running through my head, every
phone rang, I tell myself it's not him,
it wasn't

Me: I'm so over mydamnspace, I don't even know why I'm looking at it.
Tiff: What's up, who's on?
Kiera: Anything?
Me: Nada—all out shopping for my party.
Tiff: Brian still stalking you?
Me: Uh huh, three messages.
Tiff: Dude, you're definitely not going to let him come tonight.
Kiera: Yeah, that's the only reason he's being so psychotic.
Me: Um, thanks.
Tiff: I mean he's seriously in love with you.
Kiera: He worships you.
Me: Um, it's true, bitches, so shut up.

Throw on some stuff.

On our way out, stop to give puppy love. Some day I will rescue 99 dogs from a pound. And hire some animal lover to walk their asses. JK.

Yeah I look pretty f-ing good, don't I? For a sick girl, where's that Advil?
Want to know my secret? Hello, I am a cheerleader. We bounce back. It's all about quick rebound.

We go over the bad people again, the ones who aren't gonna come. Oh god, remember last night? Kiera says. Remember when Paula—she can't stop laughing. Yeah, Paula Ondagio—(yeah, *you*, Paula, I know you're stalking this)—came up to us all whiny and demanding, like so what if her father is the head school guidance counselor. It's so not cool that you didn't invite me, she said. *Ha!* What a loser. Category Two, says Kiera.

Our Little Code, nosy bitches:

1. Category One: The preschool prostitutes—the 14-year-olds who are totally promiscuous, slutty and stealing our guys! (And don't even know they're being used.)
2. Category Two: Wannabes like Paula Ondagio who are always in your face about where did you get your clothes and how much they want to be your personal fetish. (Not like the humble worshippers who know their place. JK.)
3. Category Three: Total bitches who we completely hate as opposed to ordinary bitches who create fun drama.

These are the ones who will *not* be there because we spent hours going over the lists and speaking of stalker/crashers who do you think just walks the f in like he doesn't notice me sitting in the freakin' window?

More dirt about last night. How Red Bull + vanilla vodka + shady spiced rum = pukefest for those who are ridiculous lightweights. Also disgusting: girl at club kept touching my butt, told her to get her freakin' hands off me. Except for that one hot guy—& Tiff's killer remedy—the night sucked. The DJ was lame, nonstop 80s and some droning electronic crap. *My* DJ is off-the-chain, seriously. If everything else sucks, I at least know the music's gonna be good. But it's not gonna suck, says Kiera. We have all the good people, says Tiff. Cheer, girls, cheer!

i still don't get w__ had to see his sorry ass and ytf __s stupid face still gave me this instant jolt. like your heart is an idiot dog thumping its tail at __e wrong person.

Me: I'm going in the bathroom to piss.
Tiff: Piss? That's ugly.
Me: What should I say, tinkle? Fuck you.
Tiff: Anyway you're just going in to fix yourself up, so hurry.
Me: For Brian? Why would I?
Kiera: Too late, here he comes.
Me: What's up.
Brian: Nothing, I want to talk to you.
Me: So talk.
Brian: Not here. Let's go in my car.
  I'll pull it up to the front.

12:30 p.m.

I'm sitting there waiting. Why?

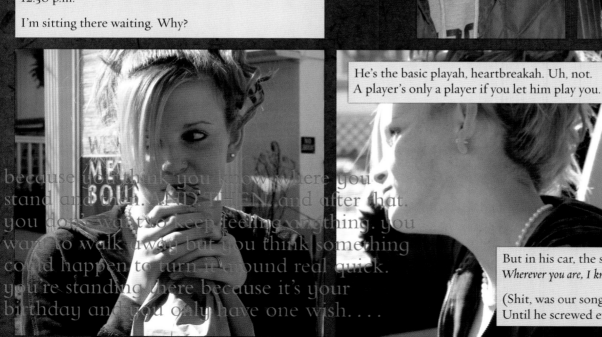

He's the basic playah, heartbreakah. Uh, not.
A player's only a player if you let him play you.

because you think you know where you
stand and then AND THEN and after that.
you don't want to keep feeling anything. you
want to walk away but you think something
could happen to turn it around real quick.
you're standing there because it's your
birthday and you only have one wish. . . .

note to self:
next time you
have a song
with someone,
pick some
obscure hit
from Finland.

But in his car, the song is blastin':
Wherever you are, I know you can feel me.

(Shit, was our song until last week.
Until he screwed everything up.)

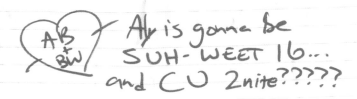

AB + BW

Ally is gonna be SUH-WEET 16... and CU 2nite?????

Hey I'm sorry, he says. Come on.

Shut up.

But I miss you.

Too late. Should've thought of that before.

(They always want you back right before a party.)

What are you going to wear, he says.

When are you going to stop being gay, I say.

Happy birthday, he says.

I gotta go, I say.

Where you going?

To do my hair.

Why—you already look so perfect and beautiful and perfect, he says.

(Okay, okay, he didn't say that, but the dude was freakin' thinking it, just look at that face. His loss.)

in the car where we'd spent so much time, I almost gave in. it would've been so easy to fall back into his game. he had that vulnerable look that was so hard to resist. he put his hand on me and said my name so quietly. I jerked my hand away, but I wanted to let him pull me back in . . . keeping that cool attitude, slamming the door of his car, watching him drive off. and the whole time not letting anyone know what i was going through. act tough even if you don't feel it and eventually it will be real.

There's Nik and Lauryn and the rest of their clique.

i thrive on pressure of certain kinds. i need to be the best. you're always checking someone else out—what does she have, is it as good as mine, look at her hair, what's she got on her feet, how does she mix the new trends with the classic pieces—how pretty is her face, how hot is her attitude—and then you get that click inside, you ALWAYS get that click, it's like a coin falling into a slot, like a shooting star landing in my heart, and it says: YOU'RE BETTER. it's like a game and you do it automatically unless the stakes are high, like the day of your 16th effin birthday and then your heart is racing because this time it's for real, you have to be better.

1 p.m.

It might look like torture to you, but this is how I do my private meditation and prayer ritual, fuck you if you don't believe in God.

It's not cool to admit this, but the whole reason boys like skinny eyebrows is they like to think of the suffering and pain hotties go through. Don't look at me like that, and btw even unibrows need weeding, so you're next, dudettes.

um, i was not exactly chill. was in high gear even with eyes closed.
the buildup for the party was like preparing for a meet; you can't be thinking what if it's no good. you need that adrenaline because when you're pumped there's no room for doubt.

Go ahead and drop $100 on those sunglasses (that I bought a month ago, in black and in white) but you know you're not going to rock them like me.

Go ahead and pick through those sale racks, not one of you's gonna find what I got—

A dress actually worn by Paris during a sample show in . . . Paris. Not a copy of it, but *it*, the dress. It was on her *skin*. It touched her *molecules*. And it's poppin', you wouldn't even get it. If you saw it you'd prolly walk on by it . . . .

paris hilton is not my hero, but if you flash on her attitude it can get you through things. you basically know PH would not get up in the morning and start crying, saying oh god, who am i. i'm such a loser, no one loves me, oh god i exposed my bare butt at that fashion show and now it's going to be in all the papers, i'm like soooo embarrassed. well maybe she does wake up feeling like that, but she doesn't let it show, or if she lets it show she'll make it look cute, she'll make it work, she'll turn it around and be smiling by breakfast. THAT is the attitude i keep in mind when i feel like things are breaking down. so having her actual dress is cool.

8 p.m.

My only shot in the limo. And it doesn't even come out. Well we were not lookin' real pretty anyway, lots of: Where's that Visine, and dude, your eyes are gonna clash with your dress. Getting close to the grand entrance and my girls more pumped than me. Let's take care of that disconnect. This is the good part when you know you're gonna get there, and stay there and basically fly through the whole thing, buzzing like a bee, until you land the next day and get to say, yeah I made it. So suck it up and keep it in until it comes around again.

And where is the shot of my big moment, the moment when the whole night's out on the curb waiting for you? (*Late birthday hint for those who gave me lame presents:* Send me shots of us in the limo when we got out and all the flashes were poppin'!)

Okay I'm being a biatch, these guys are my friendz 4real, but they gotz to know I am the queeeeeeeeen!

So you havin' any guest celebs there? says Nik.
Yeah, Tiff says, putting on the voice of one of those reality sweet sixteen babes: Her Daddy promised her Kanye, riding in bareback on Damian Marley's shoulders, both of them singing "I'm N Luv (Wit a Stripper).
And don't forget the triple level olympic size jacuzzi, says Kiera, with the overhead tanning lights.

DAMIAN MARLEY—random!?

And her dad for real got her a fog machine, light show, RSVP seating chart, and DJ DIVA Irie DeVINE, says Nik.

Woo-hoo! say the happy shoppers.
Can't wait.
Excitement builds.

Cheer, my girls, cheer!
Queen exits.

funny, no shots inside the limo, what a mystery. . . . tiff was so high from some shit she got off her brother that she couldn't stop laughing. somebody pimp slap me, she said, which made her laugh even more. we made her down some handy red bull, as if that would get her normal! it was pretty sick. when it was time to get out i had this surreal feeling like: is this really it and why wasn't i feeling it more? the buildup's so big—you expect that one moment to be perfect, instead this feeling of almost dread like you've got to put on this huge performance that's supposedly all about you and your good time—but you're doing the whole show for everyone else. but fuck it, you dive in anyway.

I love dancing with my girls just as much. Everyone's here, even the kids I don't hang out with. But everyone who's ever said hey to me and not had an attitude, they're here if they want to be.

It's all a blur, it's dark enough for things to blend, when you're high enough to make amends/pass that pipe
When every girl is your friend/we're so connected/we're so eclectic/we can really talk/pass that pipe
I've got an herbal remedy/for every freakin' malady/
At least for tonight/
Tomorrow it will all go back/to being what it was/rejected/dejected/you're only as big as who you know/
But now/we're so connected

actually, finland is too close to hom

Now that song is just raw accuracy. Not about me, you understand. I was not the one spewing Skittle-colored chunks into the f-ing bathroom sink. (That would be Meghan Ryland.)

Party. *Mardi fuckin' Gras.*

Everything happening here, even live goldfish swimming around in martini glasses on every table.

Know what I want?
Him? Nah.

Know what I want? To have fun.
Know what I want? What I want. Whatever it is.
Don't you?

Maybe him.   Maybe him.   Maybe him.

guys i've known all my life, all of them going to martin luther king high. how exciting. Did we hook up? Nah, it's never worth it. Well, sometimes, but you got to choose your battles.
brian goes to study . . . STFU! if you drink enough you'll dissolve any boy from the last corner of your mind.

then kristyn, dancing up close to me, whisper-shouting in my ear: so i guess brian's not happening?
shut up bitch, i know you hooked up with jaz's boyfriend like two seconds after they broke up. you gonna go after brian now? but didn't say this like i did. why f-ing leave people out? even losers need to party, but was it that obvious that he wasn't there? would have to try harder to show everyone that i didn't freak n care.
tiff was like: was that bitch messing with you? what is wrong with you?
and i'm: nothing a little of that can't cure.
tiff: well then here's a little of that.
me: know what i'm saying?
tiff: i know.
but she didn't really know . . . the music, the drink and all the attention were not wiping the stress of the pill.

1 a.m.

There's a few tiny off-the-chain incidents—like Adam Morgenstern being all stoned on his brother's painkillers and obviously letting everyone know by trying to turn our "Milkshake" choreography into a moshpit.

Here's the part you all have been waiting for—my top three awards for the night (no prizes, greed hags):

1. Most Times Caught Tipping That Sketchy Infused Vodka Into My Virgin Punchbowl Out of That Nasty Flask That Looks Like She Stole It From a Homeless Person: Anastasia Morelli.

(What next, liquid heroin?)

2. Best Depiction of a Category One (Just out of curiosity, did you forge my invite or just do the guy at the door?) or: (Okay, you might see me as a desperate crasher/loser/stalker, but inside me lurks a party animal who's not afraid to wear something I found in the dumpster.): Kylie Verdan.

3. Best Impersonation of a Stripper: Tanya Michaels. (Um, Tan, honey, when you have kankles, you really don't want to try and hide them by putting them behind your head while dancing.)

And here's a few candid shots (like you didn't know there were cameras!)

So did I hook up with anyone?
Hey, out of my business, ho! If I want to tell you, you'll know, aight?

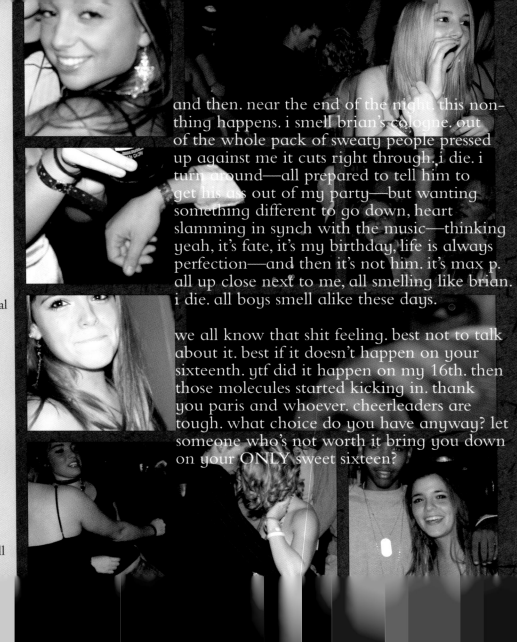

and then. near the end of the night. this non-thing happens. i smell brian's cologne. out of the whole pack of sweaty people pressed up against me it cuts right through. i die. i turn around—all prepared to tell him to get his ass out of my party—but wanting something different to go down, heart slamming in synch with the music—thinking yeah, it's fate, it's my birthday, life is always perfection—and then it's not him. it's max p. all up close next to me, all smelling like brian. i die. all boys smell alike these days.

we all know that shit feeling. best not to talk about it. best if it doesn't happen on your sixteenth. ytf did it happen on my 16th. then those molecules started kicking in. thank you paris and whoever. cheerleaders are tough. what choice do you have anyway? let someone who's not worth it bring you down on your ONLY sweet sixteen?

I love it when it's finally happening,
the music *is* your brain. Your mind free.
Shit, says Teryn, the DJ keeps playin'
yours and Brian's song.

Wherever you are, I know you can feel me.
I know you can feel all the things going through me.

Yeah, he keeps playing it.
Just like I asked him to.

Know what I wanted? I wanted you.
I get what I want. I always do.
When I don't want you anymore
You'll know we're through.

Cos it's my song now.

Wherever you are, I know you can feel me
I know you can feel all the things
                    going through me

Know what I wanted? I wanted you.
I get what I want. I always do.
When I don't want you anymore
            You'll know we're through.

The

65c
IN CANADA 75c

Romance of

Tristan

and →CHLOE

Iseult

ANCHOR
A2

AS RETOLD BY

they'll turn my reality into a story
that stretches into nowhere, twisting
it until it snaps, but i won't be able
to set them straight. haven't you
ever had it, i'll want to scream.
haven't you ever had real love?

TOMORROW

there will be messages back and forth and bits of tonight
will become ugly fragments, spit out all over the internet.

did you hear that chloe and tristan hooked up?
they spent the night together at rachel's house!

what about rachel, does she know?

duh, who do you think told me?
she got up in the middle of the night and saw
them sleeping together on the freakin' couch!

is chloe grounded or did she lie to her mom again?
i heard she's been on the pill since she was 11. jk.

TOMORROW

as soon as i walk in the door, my mom will be out of control, because she always is. this love will become a dark and raw battle we'll have in the hallway before i can get into my room and collapse on my bed.

was rachel's brother home last night? you didn't sneak into his room, did you? i know how that mother is, she doesn't believe in rules. did that mother cook anything for you, she never cooks, that one. what do you mean you cooked, you never cook, why don't you ever have your friends over here and cook, why does everyone have to hang out at rachel's, are you ashamed of me, of your house? i want to trust you, chloe, damn it, look at me.

her words will turn the honey in my heart into hardness.

look at me, i'm worried about you, something about this doesn't feel right, are you doing drugs? did you protect yourself? why can't i meet him? make sure he respects you, do you know that boys sometimes just do this for fun and they'll tell you anything?

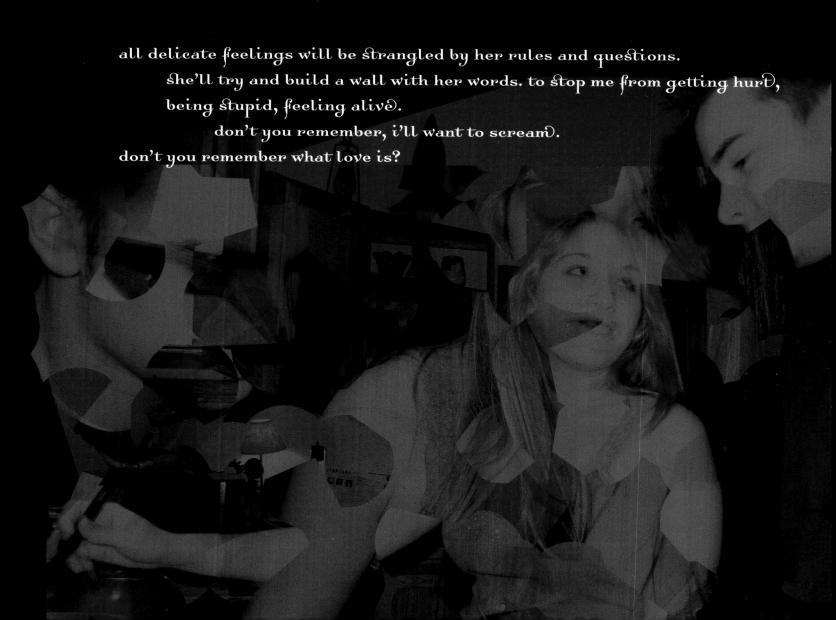

all delicate feelings will be strangled by her rules and questions.

she'll try and build a wall with her words. to stop me from getting hurt,

being stupid, feeling alive.

don't you remember, i'll want to scream.

don't you remember what love is?

TOMORROW

i'll tell my closest friends the basics:

i spent the night at rachel's house, and rachel's boyfriend TJ was there. and yeah, she has a cool mom, who just lets us chill. yeah, i hung out with tristan again and he was so cute—he gave me this little book, just some book he got for a quarter at the flea market. but it's called tristan and iseult. right, we were studying it last year, we had to see that boring movie. only tristan, he crossed out the—he drew a little animal inside—here, i'll show you. see? he's just so cute. we ate pasta, i cooked it.

we watched TV and me and tristan basically fell asleep on the couch.
there's something about that couch and the glow of the TV—
it always puts me out.

i'll tell my friends some details, i'll show them the book.
they'll see my face and know the whole story.

BUT TOMORROW HASN'T HAPPENED YET

and now, in this moment,
lying on the couch in tristan's arms,
things are passing through my mind
that i will share with no one.

it's the middle of the night
and i have this feeling
like i have been breathing
in someone else's dreams.
tristan is asleep, totally quiet.
the night is so still
and i'm so awake.

i flash on tristan and iseult's love—
passionate, short, magical,
doomed, violent and tainted by outsiders.
in the end it killed them. i feel their story
waking up inside me, beating in my heart.

what if tristan & iseult's story didn't end tragically,
if their love hadn't been killed by harsh judgment.

they'd be lying together, asleep.
they'd open their eyes and say:
wow, we survived all that—now what?

and then they'd be kissing. . . .

HOW TO SURVIVE A SOLO WEEKEND

SATURDAY, NOON

Wake up late.
First thought: Aly's bad-ass sweet 16!
Tonight!
Next thought: Mom's already gone.
(For the whole weekend, WOO-
HOO!)—I start throwing on some
stuff—ALY'S PARTY! TONIGHT!—
I slam down some juice, brush my
teeth, a preview of happy images
flashing through my head: My brand-
new supercute little dress—dancing
with Ryan, that little hottie—the
crew getting ready at Nik's—the
whole weekend's going to be sick!
I'm tearing out to meet my girls
(downtown shopping) and then, on
the table by the door, I find this.

it girl

How to: **Survive
a solo weekend**
Turn your home into a spa
Get a jump on the holidays
Whip up an exotic meal
Take the focus off your troubles
Experiment with daring style
Pamper yourself

The magazine's her little joke, like—how will you manage
to survive the weekend without me? Cute, Mom, cute. (She's
already left for her conference—gone until Sunday night—YES!)
But I'll survive without you fine, and I am def not going to be solo.
The one thing everyone knows about me, is you could not pay me
to be alone.
  It's all about the crew.
  And our plans for this weekend are tight—the party, staying
over at Nik's with the crew (if we ever make it back to her house)
and of course the classic day-after, trashed-but-happy breakfast
at the diner.

Minutes later, we're all downtown, looking for the last-minute bling. I'm trying on designer shades, some over-the-top fake fur, the music in the store is SLAMMIN' and we're all doing a few moves right there, can't wait to get on the floor tonight, she's getting this hot DJ from Boston. The beats in the store are LOUD as a club, too bad they're not loud enough to drown out Nik. Now there is one opinionated bitch, giving all of us a hard time—(you don't have the money for THAT—gross, you have pit stubble—that dress makes you look pregnant)—thinking she's all sharp. But I don't want to lower my vibe by going down to her level.

Snack time. We're sitting there with our little salsa and chips and suddenly we get into it.

Do you really have to ask what it's about? It is ALWAYS about a guy. Could be ANY guy.

But THIS ONE has a way of looking at you STILL and DEEP, THIS ONE smells soooooooo good stands REAL CLOSE to you in the HALLS close enough so you don't CARE what he's actually SAYING (even though it's likely some playah play).

And THIS one happens to be RYAN. The one supposed to hook up with ME at Aly's PARTY and here's NIK telling me (on the DAY of the party) that I'm BRAINDEAD (her exact word, and she's said it before) BRAINDEAD (her little joke about me since we were in junior high and I used to write poems) and I'm BRAIN-DEAD (she says) cos Ryan's been HITTING on HER (she says) but we ALL know that is a LIE, we ALL know that SHE has likely been HITTIN' on him because that is her COMPETITIVE BOY-STEALING BACK-STABBING PHONY-ASS IGNORANT STYLE but we all just deal with it only now I CAN'T but THEY can so she gets in my face and I give it back but no one else does and then—they ditch me.

Brutal. Did not see this one coming. They will be back. They'll be missing me. No way they can shop without me livening things up.

They WILL be back. Only—they're not.

Bright idea: I could catch up with them. He's just a guy. There's always another. Only I really like him. And hate them.

Bright idea #2: They're trying to bring me down—but I'm gonna bounce back. I'm gonna go right into that cute boutique, get what I need for the party. But—shopping alone! All shaky and desperate in the dressing room, with the fake preppy bitches checking you out and making their little judgments. I know half those girls, they'll be at Aly's party tonight. They're probably all like—what's Lauryn doing without her crew? Try a different store? Hell no. Besides, I'm all set for the party, been set for weeks. So I head home.

4:30 p.m.

To find that magazine again.

My mother is a psychic witch. Did she put a spell on me to make me stay home? Nothing else could keep me here. Last time I spent the night alone was exactly NEVER. Last time I missed a big party was the night I was grounded back when I was 13 and everyone else got drunk at Tiffany Allen's bat mitzvah bash. Aly's party is going to make that one look like a preschool picnic. Aly's party's going to be fierce, all Mardi Gras, that DJ from Boston who's supposed to be the shit. Aly's party is the only thing that got me through this whole month of school. I am so GOING to that party, with or without them.

5:30 p.m.

So then why am I sitting here frozen on the bed, one hour later, looking at this thing? Thinking they might call. I'll go check the computer, like a loser.

I knew it—back and forth, they're all talking about what time they're meeting and where.

Tamara's already at Nik's place. Savannah needs to borrow some silver pumps, she's asking Lindsie W. if she has some. Yeah, because I was gonna lend them to her, biatch, and no one else has a size ten.

Nothing about me. Shit, I had the best outfit. And Ryan was saying that shit about save all the dances for him. I am NOT shooting them an instant message. I want to go so bad. I could jump in, be right back in the game. Hell no. Let them miss me.

6:30 p.m.

Well, better start gettin' ready. Any second now. Why am I lying here? You know why. Because your palms are sweating. Your heart is racing. Can't even shop without my crew. How am I going to go to a party alone? The crew MAKES the party—always someone to dance with, inside jokes, know they'll back you up. We don't even go to the bathroom without each other. And Ryan and his crew will think I'm a freak if I suddenly show up alone. Who am I kidding, the party is out—unless I –

Score, they're calling!

Damn, only Mom, checking in.

Why don't you ask one of your

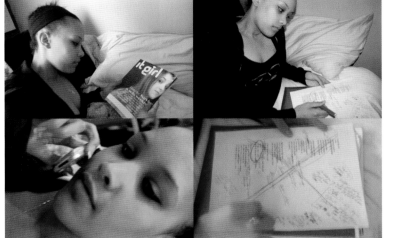

other friends to go to the party with you? Mom wants to know. You know so many girls, she says. You don't need Nik.

Does she not get it that you don't randomly hook up with other people to go to a party this big, at the last minute? There are types that do that (Nik), that push their way through things (Nik) and have the confidence to hook up with anyone and show up anywhere like they deserve to be there. Nik, Nik, Nik.

And then there are types who would never do that—even though they're always up for a good time, for hanging with the girls. That would be me.

But I'm NOT a SHEEP! NOT a FOLLOWER! I've NEVER been scared of Nik like the rest of them. Until now, I have been SPOILED, because people have always been calling me, always there, never had to worry about being the one to start something up. And never had to face every single bitch bailing. Well at least you have that magazine for survival tips, Mom says brightly.

6:45 p.m.

Going through my party things that had been arranged carefully on hangers, on my dresser—do NOT need to stare at them all night, start shoving them in a drawer. In the back of the drawer is an archaelogical strata of my existence—the porn cartoon John M. did last year and passed me in art class (it's perverted but shows talent), the magic kit from when I was obsessed with magic in the ninth grade, a set of glitter lip glosses, all dried up from eighth grade and—the poem. From last week. Written on my computer. Way too long. Not enough intensity. Not from the heart. Too many words. I take out a pen. I pretend to be pulled in by the poem.

The fucking poem.

7:00 p.m.

So Chels calls. Like 20 minutes before they are leaving for the party. Almost don't take it but then I do.

Hey, Chelsea says. Hear excited laughter from the rest of the crew, coming from another room. Shit! I hear Tamara squealing, you look like a stripper! I'm right in there almost, already smilling, who looks like a stripper, I almost say, only I know it's probably Zoey, I know the exact shoes she's wearing, we picked them out together—I am supposed to BE THERE WITH THEM.

Lauryn, you were soooo out of control, Chelsea says.

This red streak of rage slices through me, did not expect her to do me dirty like that, but she's been backing up Nik all the time since Nik's house became the partyhouse. So I push it down. Yeah, okay, I say. I can see the crew, all squeezed into Nik's sloppy bathroom, fighting over that long mirror, balanced on the edge of the tub, craning for a spot—I need to be there. Could be there still if I play it right.

Chelsea's going on: you were like practically psychotic.

But what about Nik, I say. You were there. Did you not see Nik getting in my face. Did you not hear what she was saying about Ryan hitting on her?

Get over it, Chels says. You are so freakin' unnecesarily sensitive.

But I was gonna hook up with Ryan. This is barely even true, so why am I clinging to it.

Chels is quiet for a beat and then she says: so then call him.

What. Are. You. Saying. My voice comes out clipped and even, matching her coolness, even though I've got alarms going off inside.

Since Ryan's your whole focus, maybe you should go to the party with him, the bitch says.

You know I am not going to do that, you know that's not my style—I get this random flash of Ryan, and the idea of calling him the night of the party is like science fiction, it's so out of the realm of reality—and Chelsea knows it, she's just playing me and I'm letting her—damn, I am letting her!

But surprise—Chels softens.

Look, just talk to Nik, she's in the other room, I'll put her on. She's the old Chels again, my pal, wanting me to be there, it woud be so easy. Come on, Ryan's nothing, he's probably going to hit on Aly anyway, since she broke up with what's-his-name—and you're ruining our plans, we're going to make an entrance.

There's this little pause and then her voice gets even softer and sweeter, like a mom coaxing an unreasonable child: You know you're not going to blow off this party, Lauryn.

Instead of pulling me in this time, her words twist in my stomach. We've been here before. How many years have we been here before. The moment where one of them takes Nik's side. The moment where I suck it up.

You know what? I say. Screw you.

And click off the phone.

7:14 p.m.

So what I do then is panic.

The whole idea that I'm not going is like a big sheet of glass sitting in my stomach. And the only thing to do with that big undigestible piece of glass is to eat. I stand with the fridge hanging open suddenly needing to grab anything to shove the feelings down.

But there's nothing to eat cos Mom thought I'd be at the party. I'm alone in the house with nothing to eat, the party about to happen, sweaty palms and dry mouth. I go in my room and I'm alone in my room, the sun going down, all of them OUT, probably already high, and I'm standing here alone in the silence, not wearing the $18 white tea flavored lip gloss in a shade called violently happy oh yeah, I'm violently happy being here, holding the new bottle of the Dolce and Gabbana light blue perfume that cost $45 so I could feel Ryan up close to me when we were dancing at Aly's party, feel him breathing in my light blueness. I'm standing here like a lame wasted freak, letting the bottle catch the light from my lamp, and wanting to CRASH it to the floor but who wants the room soaked in the scent of LOSER because I am too afraid to get myself dressed—I still could do that—could get myself dressed and get a cab, I am so feeling the beats, that Boston DJ, I want to hear some Spleen, that Ciara song, some REGGAETON, anything. I was going to dance—maybe I will, maybe I'll go there alone, show up alone, I can do it, it's not illegal—I was going to rock that criss-cross low cut thin black no back perfect fucking dress just like the one J.Lo wore on TRL not that I like her but the dress, damn it, the dress. It was going to be sick.

WE were going to be in it together, we were going to be WE and now it's THEM out there being wild and me trapped here with this magazine and its tips that would be good if you had the IQ of a ripe banana. I don't know why I said ripe banana except that is all there is in this house. (Aly said there was going to be jambalaya and ribs and chicken and pizza at the party.) Yeah, all we have is a bowl of brown fruit with tiny flies over them and other than that there is a $20 bill and it doesn't take long to get to the store and spend it on what I will need for the night if I decide not to commit suicide or smash everything up in my room. Karma is a bitch and they'll get the payback some day.

7:30 p.m.

I start out the door for food but I'm shaking so bad I can't even turn the door knob, I have to get it out somehow, get it out, I'm stamping through the house yelling BITCHES and the old lady upstairs is pounding her broom handle, the witch, to make me shut up, and I go in my room and take out my diary because I have to scream the pain out, I have to tell someone, and I take my red pen and I start to write about how much I hate those bitches and how it's the worst night of my life and I'm wiping my wet face on my hands and the page is blurred but I keep going but then instead of a diary thing what I'm writing is this rageful poem.

I keep writing and then the words start to be interesting and I play with them and it takes a long time to move them around but I don't even notice the time, and then I look at the clock and I look at what I've written—and it's short and it's strong and it says what I really feel, but the store's almost closing and I'm really hungry now and not shaking at all so I grab the money and run out the door.

8:40 p.m.

I check the caller ID and did not miss their call while I was out buying supplies. And I'm getting through, I don't need those bitches, I have this mangy creature.

I have this food I'm shoving in my mouth without tasting, glad no one can see me I look

like the devil. Junk food is grim and TV's no fun without the crew. Hey cat, do you like being in Loserville with me, watching Tyra Banks all raising her eyebrows at that poor girl from Tennessee? Do you know that I feel abnormal and raw inside now that we both know I can barely survive, whatever this is, this being alone. Do I miss them, Do I really need them to even make reality TV seem more real? Am I not changing into my PJs or even taking off my shoes because I can't even get that I'm still here. That it is so quiet. That when the dimness of the room brightens with the headlights of passing cars it makes me feel so lonely.

I do not feel this fist grinding down into my chest, like they pushed across all miles and broke through all matter so they could make me feel this bad while they are out partying. They cannot touch me. I could still go, but I spent the $20, so there won't be a cab.

3:00 a.m.

In the middle of the night a tire screech wakes me, a screech and a surge of bass from someone's radio, can almost feel the laughter and good times in the car, and it all gets inside me like a bad dream. And then I fall asleep again. Deeply asleep.

I dream I go into the tattoo shop and I'm trying to pick out a design and I'm all excited, like how about a tramp stamp? How about all that ink running into your skin broken by a needle like the guy on the table wincing with pleasure, no thanks, besides I don't want ink on my body, maybe on my hands, tell the world how I feel every time I make a fist, love with one fist, hate with another, or do I want a cartoon mated to me for life, a unicorn on my back or a monkey, no thanks and besides I don't have any money. Only I don't get a tattoo.

I'm suddenly at the park and at first it's scary and sad.

I'm waiting for my friends and I feel like I'm three and I'm realizing they're never gonna come, I'm realizing I missed the party and it's the

others laughing gives them pain and forces them to bang the floor with brooms, like witches and here she is laughing with her friend and I actually go into the kitchen to find a broom so I can be the one to ram the floor with it, that's how crazy I am this morning.

But in the kitchen I find more junk to take to bed, oh yeah, it's a fresh and sparkling start to a new and gorgeous day. the party over, missed it all,

The world empty of friends, time to put on my PJs and get into bed and get ready to say good morning God!, what do you have planned for us next, how would you like me to serve you and your depressing, twisted world?

Who are the low-down, predictable people in your neighborhood, in your neigborhood, who are the—time to turn off the Sunday sermons and kiddie TV.

Another round of things to get me through the morning.

I feel like puking. I am such a slob. No I'm not, I'm just a person. A nice person. I, Lauryn, am a noble being! But they would think I was a slob. Glad they can't see me. More glad I don't have to see their phony-assed nasty faces. Maybe I will move to Los Angeles and live a life of soft, beachy nights and be discovered on a beach. Maybe Ryan missed me last night even if they didn't. But I bet they did. Ha!

Not too late to get a tattoo, for real!

10:00 a.m.

And then suddenly I remember. That fierce little poem. Probably not as good as I thought. I open my diary and read it. Again and again. It makes my heart beat in my throat. I don't know if it's good but it might be. It makes me feel strong.

So they've got their little hangovers and their day-after chit-chat (I MISSED EVERYTHING AND I HATE THEM AND MY LIFE SUCKS) but I've got this poem (I SHOULD BE THERE FOR THE DAY AFTER

next day. Then I climb up into this tower and the dream gets all tropical and colorful and fun. And I sit in this tower which is suddenly just a plastic kiddie playthingie (you know how dreams are) and inside are all these notes written to me from RYAN. And it feels really cool and it's like he's written me all these beautiful love poems. I'm happy but then I read them closely and they're just stupid pieces of graffiti, really stupid, things like CALL ME HOTTIE (you know how dreams are). And I'm leaving the woods and I have my purse on and I feel stupid and I wake up.

SUNDAY, 9:00 a.m.

I wake because it's daylight and the TV's still on and I slept in my clothes on the floor. I wake because the old lady upstairs is laughing with company, she never has company, she always hits the floor with a broom handle when my crew is over and I have the music too loud and Mom says old people get enraged with jealousy because they are so lonely and the sound of

CHIT-CHAT AND DID I MENTION EXACTLY HOW much MY LIFE IS
SHIT) but I've got this poem and only one more day of this nasty weekend
to get through, and when Monday comes, fucking Monday, I'm under no
illusion this poem won't save me. I'll still be dealing with fucking Nik and
them when Monday comes, the ugliest day of the week, Monday. When it
comes Nik will still be a bossy bitch and Ryan will still catch me in the hall
and I'll be the only one of them who knows how hard it is to be alone and
I'll just have to see exactly how high you can bounce when you're back.

THE END

I UNPLUGGED THE MACHINE
TO SEE WHAT WOULD HAPPEN
IF I STARTED BREATHING
ON MY OWN

ALONE
TO FACE WHAT I OWN
BENEATH SKIN AND BONES
THIS PEN IS MY NEEDLE
BLOOD IS MY INK
I WILL LEAVE MY MARK ON THIS PAGE

THE TATTOO IS WHAT I
CHOOSE TO SHOW YOU

DIG DEEPER IF PAIN
DOESN'T SCARE YOU
GO BEYOND SKIN & BONES

FIND MY HEART
LOUD, CONNECTED TO YOURS
BEATING ON ITS OWN

baby it girl

Because of my dad's job, we move a lot. Every time you go to a new school, it's the same thing:

1. You have to find out what clothes are cool and how people wear their hair.

2. Everyone wants to be your friend and you have to choose—or no one wants to be your friend and it's embarassing because you have to do everything alone.

So I went into this new school a few months ago and on the bus, this girl Abbie asked me if I wanted to play with her at recess. I said sure.

And then in homeroom, two perfect-looking girls started telling me how to fix my hair— you had to pull it back and up, really tight, to make it perfectly smooth. They told me to get a certain kind of clip at Claire's at the mall and to practice at home.

Then the girls asked me if I wanted to play with them at recess and I said sure, but I was also going to hang out with this girl Abbie, from my bus.

And they were like—Abbie? She's a mess, look at her, look at her clothes, look at her hair.

So then I had to choose.

hi, it's me, DAKOTA. KEEP IT REAL. (even if this shot seems a little fake. come on, i could have worn my baby phat sweater. i could have been raising my fist in a radical demo. i could have just had a bear walk through the back door and straight into my house. i did! i chased it away! THIS REALLY HAPPENED!) WILD MUSIC WITH STRONG BEATS PLAYED LOUD IN A FAST BLACK CAR, u do know what i am saying. my daughters (<333333) are NOBLE BEINGS. FAITH OVER FEAR and jalapeños over anything. the miracle is YOU get to decide what matters and then decide again to do it.

Atheneum Books for Young Readers » An imprint of Simon & Schuster Children's Publishing Division » 1230 Avenue of the Americas, New York, New York 10020 » Copyright © 2007 by Dakota Lane » All rights reserved, including the right of reproduction in whole or in part in any form. » Book design by Michael McCartney » Manufactured in China » 10 9 8 7 6 5 4 3 2 1 » Library of Congress Cataloging-in-Publication Data » Lane, Dakota. » The secret life of it girls / Dakota Lane.—1st ed. » p.   cm. » "Ginee Seo books." » Summary: A series of vignettes in which high school girls in a clique thresh out everything from teenage pregnancy and indiscretions on the Internet to the correct procedure for failing a Spanish exam. » ISBN-13: 978-1-4169-1492-1 » ISBN-10: 1-4169-1492-7 » [1. Cliques (Sociology)—Fiction. 2. Popularity—Fiction. 3. Interpersonal relations—Fiction.] I. Title. » PZ7.L231785Sec 2007 » [Fic]—dc22   2006019886

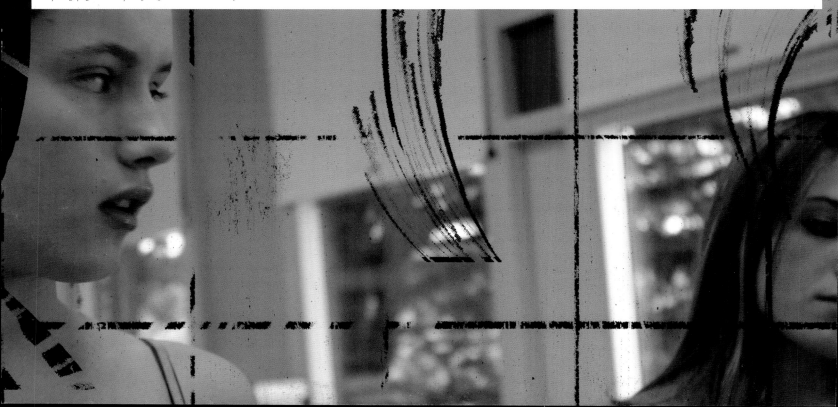